tim

BLADE

BREAKING FREE

Blade has touched the edge of death. His injuries
have left him exposed—and vulnerable.
Now his enemies have tracked him down, and he
knows they'll show no mercy.
If he doesn't get away, he's dead.
But he's weak. And he doesn't know what scares him
more . . . breaking free from those hunting him—or
breaking free from his own past.

The third title in this ground-breaking series from
Tim Bowler, the Carnegie Medal-winning author
of *River Boy*, *Starseeker*, and *Frozen Fire*. Blade is in
more danger than ever before—and it will take all
his resources to survive this time . . .

Other Books by Tim Bowler

tim bowler

winner of the carnegie medal

BREAKING FREE

book

OXFORD
UNIVERSITY PRESS

OXFORD
UNIVERSITY PRESS

Great Clarendon Street, Oxford OX2 6DP

Oxford University Press is a department of the University of Oxford.
It furthers the University's objective of excellence in research, scholarship,
and education by publishing worldwide in

Oxford   New York

Auckland   Cape Town   Dar es Salaam   Hong Kong   Karachi
Kuala Lumpur   Madrid   Melbourne   Mexico City   Nairobi
New Delhi   Shanghai   Taipei   Toronto

With offices in

Argentina   Austria   Brazil   Chile   Czech Republic   France   Greece
Guatemala   Hungary   Italy   Japan   Poland   Portugal   Singapore
South Korea   Switzerland   Thailand   Turkey   Ukraine   Vietnam

Oxford is a registered trade mark of Oxford University Press
in the UK and in certain other countries

© Tim Bowler 2009

The moral rights of the author have been asserted

Database right Oxford University Press (maker)

First published 2009

British Library Cataloguing in Publication Data

Data available

ISBN: 978-0-19-275558-2

1 3 5 7 9 10 8 6 4 2

Printed in Great Britain by CPI Cox and Wyman, Reading, Berkshire

Paper used in the production of this book is a natural,
recyclable product made from wood grown in sustainable forests.
The manufacturing process conforms to the environmental
regulations of the country of origin.

For Rachel
with my love

Ever wondered where you go when you're dead? Then watch this space. Cos I've been there. And here's something to blitz your mind.

I'm still there.

And I might not be coming back.

It's out of my control now. I can't make anything happen in this place. It's just me and Death. And you don't mess with him. He's the gobbo in charge.

But what's it like? I'll tell you, Bigeyes.

First up, no lights or heavenly voices. None of that

stuff. What you get is memories. It's just like they say. They come flashing past. They're like pictures.

They're doing it now. Pictures of people, places, stuff you've done. Your life like a movie spinning through you. And that's where it hurts.

Cos I don't want to see mine.

Or most of it. Maybe bits. The times with Becky.

Now don't get confused, cos there's two Beckys, right? Sweet and sour. There's the one who died. That's sweet Becky. And there's the one who should have died. The sour one—the troll, the dreg.

The one who zipped me over and told me little Jaz was her daughter when she wasn't. I got lots of names for that troll. But we'll call her Bex, all right? So you don't get stumped in the head. Cos you get stumped easy, don't you, Bigeyes?

Becky and Bex, sweet and sour. Got it?

I've been seeing pictures of sweet Becky. Her beautiful face, those eyes. Her hair used to shine. Did I ever tell you that? And it had this kind of smell. Sort of fragrant.

Even the day she died she smelt like a flower. And looked like one.

I miss her, Bigeyes. She's the only picture I want to see in all these memories. But I got no choice about that. I got to deal with the rest of 'em too. And they're coming thick as rain. Death's one busy gobbo.

And here's something else.

They don't all make sense. It's weird, Bigeyes. All this stuff, all these pictures—they're kind of cloudy. I thought everything would be clear in Death's little snug.

But it's not clear at all. I'm seeing things I remember and yet I don't remember. Does that make sense? Like they're memories but they're not. Things I've done only I've forgotten.

Specially the early stuff.

That's the stuff that's really hard to see. I can see bits but lots of it's sort of shadowy, like it's almost a memory but not quite. Maybe that's a good thing. I've never liked remembering.

But at least it's not jumping about. It comes in the right order. Starts with Day One. And here's the first problem. Cos Day One's a shadow. Can't remember Day One, can't see it clear. But I can feel it. And that's the second problem.

Cos it was trouble. I'm telling you, it was trouble.

That's right, Bigeyes. The bad stuff started on Day
One.

Don't ask me how I know.

And the pictures keep coming. Age one, age two,
age three and on they go. I don't like to watch 'em but
they keep coming. They just won't stop. He's one mean
gobbo, this Death.

Age seven.

I'm standing on the pedestrian crossing, stopping
all the traffic, swearing at the drivers. Only now, when
I see it flashing in front of me, it's not like I remember
it. What's different is me.

I'm different.

Cos I'm not just a seven-year-old kid in this picture. I'm a kid who's lived for seven years. And that's
not the same thing at all. Not when I've just watched
those seven years again and seen what's in 'em, and
who's in 'em, and what happened.

And there's shadows in there too, stuff I can't see,
stuff I've blocked out and don't want to remember. Or
maybe it's stuff that's blocked me out. Don't know.
Doesn't make much difference.

It's bad anyway.

I'm seeing that kid on the pedestrian crossing like I'm watching someone I never knew before. Only there's no time to think about it. Cos there's more pictures coming.

Age eight, and then the change, the big change. If it was bad before, it's worse now. New places, new faces, new dangers. Big new dangers. Only I'm getting dangerous too. You better believe it. I'm getting dangerous too.

And I'm starting to like it.

Age nine, age ten. It changes again. I meet Becky, sweet Becky. Good pictures at last, only more dangers too, more faces. I can see most of 'em now. Not many shadows here. It's the stuff before seven that's cloudy. This later stuff's easy to see.

And I don't like it.

I almost prefer the shadows. They're bad news but at least I can't see what they are. These other pictures—I can't miss 'em. Each one's like the knife Trixi's brother stung in my head.

And they're coming too fast. I want to tell Death to slow down, only I don't dare. Like I say, you don't mess with this gobbo.

Age ten. Yeah, I'm still seeing age ten. It's taking time to run through. That's cos so much happened in it. Too much. I'm starting to hurt, starting to want out. I'm starting to lose it. Only good thing is Becky.

Then I lose her too.

Age eleven. When it came to a head, when it all got too much. And then I'm gone.

Only I'm not. I've run away, left the old place far behind. I've moved to the city and I'm playing dead. I thought it was a good idea. But I should have known better. It was a dimpy idea. It worked for three years.

But they were always going to find me.

You can't play dead with these gobbos. The only dead for them is real dead. And you don't play it. Cos dead's not a game. Not with them.

The pictures keep coming. Lots of 'em now. Like the closer I get to when the knife plugged me, the better I see stuff. Maybe it's just cos it's more recent. Don't think so though. Death's not fussy how he gives you stuff. He just blams it in your face. And right now he's spinning more than I can keep up with.

There's the places in the city, places where I slapped it, living rough on the streets, before I found my snugs. Duffs I hung around with in alleys, door-ways, hovels, ruins, finding out where they went.

Then finding my own way.

The houses and flats and other places I snugged out in. I got pictures of all of 'em rushing through my head. And all the nebs I saw. The slugs I kept away from in the city, the gangs who caught up with me.

Like Trixi's lot.

And then Mary. Old white-haired Mary with her crazy dog. And here's another thing about Death, Bigeyes. He's not fair. You'd think now he's got me he'd tell me what happened in the bungalow that day.

Only no.

Like I say, he's one mean gobbo.

He shows me the house again, and the gobbos. I can see 'em forcing their way in. Paddy and his mate, and the fat man, the hairy grunt. I can see myself running away. I can hear the gunshots again.

Bang! Bang!

Two of 'em, loud in my brain. Only I still can't see what happened in the bungalow. Why won't Death show me that?

Cos he's too hot with buzzing the next picture at me. Trixi's body lying on the floor. Paddy leering in the doorway. Sour Bex smashing the window, and me and her running away.

And I still don't know what happened to Mary. Cos everything's moving again. It's me and Bex and now little Jaz. I don't know she's Trixi's daughter. Bex's told me the kid's her own. Only Bex was lying.

And the pictures keep coming. Bex disappears, Jaz disappears. I find 'em again, only I find the girl gang too. And Riff. And Dig, the big guy, Trixi's brother, the guy with the knife.

And the gobbos are still after me. Paddy's gone but there are still five left. And I'm wounded now. Dig's knife's ripped up my forehead and I'm blacking out. And here's where everything turns dark.

What do I remember at the end?

A knife moving, cool as a breeze. A hot pain singing in my head. The trolls in the girl gang screaming. Riff standing back, Dig grinning. The whole crowd bundling me onto the bank, leaving me by the river. The stumble to the warehouse, the gobbos closing in.

A thought fluttering in my head. I'm fourteen and I'm going to die.

Darkness. Then gunshots.

Bang! Bang!

Two of 'em. Like the time at the bungalow. And then the voice.

It speaks my name. The name sweet Becky gave me long ago. Only the person speaking doesn't know that name. I know that cos I recognize the voice. It's the last thing I remember before this. And I'm freaking out, Bigeyes.

Cos the voice is speaking again now. I can hear it right this moment. Speaking my name like it did before.

'Blade,' it says.

And I'm feeling this shiver.

Cos the person speaking my name is dead too.

'Blade,' says the voice.

It's Mary. Old white-haired Mary with the crazy dog. But Mary's dead.

'You're dead,' I murmur.

'As dead as you are,' comes the answer.

Silence, sort of. No more voices, just the buzz of my thoughts. Then another sound. Kind of a low rumble. Can't make it out.

'You're dead,' I say again.

She doesn't answer this time. But there's still this rumble. It's not loud, just a weird blur of a sound. Something's moving too. Maybe it's me.

It's not me. It's something else.

Only I'm moving with it.

The pictures have stopped. Just darkness now, and I'm starting to wonder about death. More darkness, more rumbling. Is this it? Am I going to lose it now? Maybe that wasn't death before. Maybe it was just the way in. And now the door's closed behind me, and there's no light inside.

Or maybe . . .

Another voice, some gobbo. He's murmuring something. No, he's not. He's shouting. Just sounds like he's murmuring cos he's a long way away. He's shouting something but I can't hear the words.

Or is it me that's far away? Cos I don't know where I am, Bigeyes. I'm blown away somewhere and

I'm scared. It's like I'm in a million pieces. They're all so tiny I can't see 'em. Or maybe there's no pieces at all. Maybe I'm nothing. Maybe I don't exist.

Then it happens. The jolt, the pain, the explosion. The blinding light in my head, the picture flooding my eyes. The inside of an ambulance, two medics leaning over me, black gobbos.

Mary.

Then darkness again and a rush of thoughts. And pain everywhere, digging into me.

'Ah!'

Someone's screaming.

'It's all right,' says a voice.

Another scream. Shit, it's me.

'It's all right,' says the voice again. 'We'll get you there.'

One of the gobbos talking. But now I can hear Mary again.

'Blade.' She's speaking soft, right in my ear. 'You're going to be OK.'

I got questions banging my head now, pricking my brain worse than the wound itself. She's used that name again. And I never told her it. What's going on?

BLADE

I'm thinking back to when the knife got me. I can see the old hulk by the river. I can see Bex tied up. I can see the girl gang. I can see Tammy and Sash, and Xen and Kat. I can see dead Trixi's brother, the big guy, Dig. And Riff, his slimy mate.

But I'm moving on already. I can see little Jaz in the cabin, screaming cos she's terrified of me. And then the knife, splitting the air, splitting my head. Blood filling my eyes. Like it's doing now.

'Blood! Blood!'

'Easy, boy.'

The man's voice again. Calm-sounding gobbo. Only what can he do? I thought I was dead. I almost was. I almost am. They won't get me out of this. I'm drifting off. They won't get me back. No way.

Another jolt, another explosion, another blinding pain.

Tight round my chest. I'm screaming, sitting up, eyes open. I'm peering at faces and they're peering back. I can see the front of the ambulance, the gobbo driving, some woman next to him, turning round. I can see the medics close, edging me back down.

And Mary.

And now more faces. Only they're not here in the ambulance. I know it. They're not real. I'm seeing Becky from the past, beautiful sweet Becky. And little Jaz. And then Bex.

'Not you, troll!' I scream.

'I'm here,' she answers.

'Not you!'

'Blade—'

It's not Bex talking. It's Mary.

And I'm slumped back again, pain still pounding. It's getting worse. I'm moaning now. Can't drift off and I want to. I want to blast out somewhere else. Don't care where. Long as it's somewhere well dead.

I can feel hands touching me. Hate that, hate hands. And they're bringing the pictures back.

'Ah!'

'We're losing him.' One of the gobbos, talking fast. 'Quick!'

More hands. Something clammed over my mouth. It's going dark again. Sound of a siren growing loud.

Growing soft.

More darkness. Voices talking all at once, but they're low now. Can't even make out the words. Just know they're talking about me. Why's the pain still there if I'm drifting off?

Cos I am drifting off.

And it's good. It's a stinger. Like when I fold up in a blanket in some snug, and I know the owners aren't coming back, and it's my house, my little place, for another few hours, and I can rest, and forget, and not be me.

Not be Blade.

So why's the pain still there? It's meant to go when you die. You lose your body, you lose your pain. But I've lost my body and I still got the pain. And it's getting worse.

Now the noises are coming back. The voices, and they're not talking low. They're yelling. And the siren. That's yelling too. Everything's yelling. Even I'm yelling. That's right. I'm yelling and yelling and yelling. Cos suddenly I know what I really want.

I want life, Bigeyes. I want it back.

And I want it now.

Black silence. That's right. Black. It's got a colour.

And everything's changed again. I'm somewhere else. Only I don't know where. All I know is it's black. And it's quiet. And I'm awake in my head. You better believe it. I'm wide awake.

I'm watching cute, listening cute.

The black silence goes on falling. No voices, no sirens, no engines. No breathing even. I listen for my own. Can't hear it. But I can feel my chest moving. And the flicker of my eyes as they search the darkness.

Nothing.

Just black silence.

And me, thinking.

I'm lying down somewhere. I've worked that out. Don't know where. In a hospital maybe. They must have been taking me somewhere in that ambulance. Got to be a hospital. Only it doesn't feel like one.

The memories have come back again. Only they're different now. Or they look different. They were rushing past me before. But maybe that's cos I was dying. Now they're just floating in my head. I can't even see 'em really. There's too much darkness. I can just feel 'em moving like clouds.

And I'm starting to wonder again if I'm dead after all.

'Blade,' says a voice.

I tense up. It's Mary speaking. And she's close.

I feel something, a hand. It's touching my arm. Don't like it. Try to move my arm, flick the thing off. It's no good. Can't shift a muscle. But the hand goes away.

And the voice comes back.

'You've been badly hurt,' she says. 'A knife slash across your forehead and very deep. The doctor says it cut your temporal artery. They've fixed that but you lost a lot of blood. Your clothes were so drenched they've had to destroy them. But at least you're alive.'

'Where am I?'

'In a hospital.'

'Who else is in the ward?'

'Just you and me.'

'No other patients?'

'No, you've got it all to yourself.'

'It's dark.'

'You've got a bandage over your eyes.'

More silence. I'm glad of that cos my brain's working again. Not fast, not yet. But it's working. And I know it's bad. I'm alive, OK. I'm in a hospital. But I can't move. So I'm still dead dung.

There's too many nebs want me grilled, Bigeyes. And don't tell me Mary's the only one who knows I'm here. What about Lenny and the grunt and the others? They got to be somewhere close.

I got to find out what happened. And I got to do it quick before I get rubbed out.

'You called me Blade,' I say.

My voice sounds like someone else's.

No answer. But I know Mary's still there. I can feel her close by. So why's she not answering? I hear a movement. Someone's joined her. I don't like this. Reach up, try and get rid of the bandage.

'Stop that.' Another voice, a woman, brisk, cheery. Got to be a nurse. 'I'll take off the bandage if you want me to. Just don't pick at it. And you're not to move your other arm at all. There's a needle in it with the drip attached.'

I don't answer. I'm just glad my arm's moving again. I thought for a moment I couldn't shift it.

'Now then,' says the woman.

Another touch on my arm, firmer than Mary. I feel

my hand placed on the bed. Then a faint light round my eyes. But not much. Even with the bandage off, it feels dark.

'Can you see us?' says Mary.

Just about. Nurse leaning over me, Mary sitting by the bed. They look like ghosts. Maybe I do too.

'Can you take off the drip?' I murmur.

Nurse shakes her head.

'We'll keep it there a bit longer. It's not essential now you're out of the high-risk zone, but we'll leave it in for the moment just to be on the safe side. So don't fiddle with it, OK?'

'How long have I been here?'

They look at each other, like they don't know which one's meant to answer. Nurse draws up a chair next to Mary. I don't want this. I want Mary on her own. I got to know what happened. And how much time I got before they come for me.

Mary answers.

'They rushed you in yesterday. Operated on you straightaway and gave you a blood transfusion. You've been unconscious most of the time since.'

It's hard keeping my eyes on 'em. The lids keep

falling down. I'm aching all over now, specially my forehead. I almost want the nurse to put the bandage back. But I can't let her. There's too much to do.

I got to think.

Yesterday, Bigeyes. I've been here since yesterday. I remember the ambulance, sort of, but not the operation. Or anything since. That's bad, I'm telling you. What's been going on while I've been lying here blacko? Who else has looked in on me apart from Mary?

And who's waiting outside for when I come out?

I got to get out of here. And I can't just blast out. First I'm not strong. Second I got to play stealth anyway. Got to sneak out. Trouble is, how weak's my body? I can move my arms and head. But what about the rest of me?

I haven't even tried standing up.

'You need to rest,' says the nurse.

'I want to talk.' I nod towards Mary. 'To her.'

'In the morning. When you've slept a bit more.'

'I want to talk to her.'

I feel my eyes close. I try to keep 'em open but it's no good. They close on their own. I hear my voice still speaking.

'I want to talk to her.'

Then Mary's voice.

'I'll talk to him for a bit. Since he wants to. If that's OK.'

'He's falling asleep,' says the nurse.

'No, I'm not,' I say.

'I'll stay with him anyway,' says Mary. 'If that's OK. Just for a few minutes.'

Sound of a chair moving. I hope it's the nurse going, not Mary. I don't open my eyes. I just wait. Hand on my arm again. Feels like it did before. It's Mary's hand. I can tell. Still don't like it but I'm glad it's there. I'm glad she's there.

I keep my eyes closed.

'Mary?'

'Yes, sweetheart?'

'Is it night-time?'

'Pretty much. Well, late evening anyway.'

'Feels dark.'

'It's certainly dark outside. Cold too, even for November.'

The hand on my arm moves, strokes the skin. I give a flick and the hand goes away.

'You don't like being touched,' she says.

I don't answer. Not sure it was a question anyway.

I'm thinking faster now. I'm tired all over but I'm not going to sleep, whatever the nurse thinks. I'm too scared for that. I got to know stuff. I got to find out what to do. And I got to find out soon or I'm cooked.

'What happened at the bungalow?' I say.

She talks quiet but not just for me. She's got secrets of her own. I remember that from the bungalow. She was keeping lots back then. I like her voice, always did. Soft, Irish. Still don't trust it though. She called me sweetheart just now but she's also called me Blade. I keep my eyes closed and listen.

'They killed Buffy,' she says. 'Those men. She was barking at them and snarling and snapping her teeth. I tried to hold her back. I knew they'd kill her if she went for them.'

'And she did.'

'Yes. I couldn't stop her. She wasn't my dog, you know. She was a stray. I picked her up on the road a few days before I met you. Or maybe she picked me up. Not sure which. We just hit it off. Suited each other, I guess. I don't think she realized how grateful I was to have a rottweiler for a friend.'

'Which one of 'em killed her?'

'The fat man.'

That must have been the gunshots, Bigeyes.

'He just pulled out a knife,' says Mary, 'and let her jump onto it.'

Shit, it wasn't the gunshots.

'I keep seeing that man's face,' she says.

So do I, Bigeyes. I'm seeing it right now. I had that grunt in front of me when I was lying outside the warehouse. I could have pissed his life away. I had a knife, just like him, and he was square on, easy plug. Could have split him with one throw.

But he's still alive. And I'm stuck here.

And I still don't know about the gunshots.

Mary's talking again.

'That's what did it. Buffy getting killed.'

She falls quiet for a moment, then goes on.

'So I pulled out my gun—'

'You what!'

'I pulled out my gun and fired it, twice. Once as they came forward, once as they ran away.'

'Christ!'

'Keep your voice down.' She lowers hers even further. 'I'm not supposed to have a gun.'

I keep my mouth shut, try to think. Don't know what to make of this woman. I knew she was zipping me over that time in the bungalow. Most of what she said was lies. But I didn't know she was dangerous.

I open my eyes again. Got to keep her in view. She's sitting close. Who the hell is she?

'Green eyes,' I murmur.

'What's that?'

'You got green eyes.'

'Can you see them in the darkness?'

'No.'

But I remember 'em, Bigeyes. And how they watched me in the bungalow. Like they're doing now. Missing nothing. Figure appears in the doorway, that nurse checking. Mary sees me looking and turns her head.

'We're almost done,' she calls out.

'Couple more minutes,' says the nurse, and leaves.

Mary looks back.

'Where'd you get a gun?' I say.

'Doesn't matter.' She pauses, like she's not sure if she wants to talk, then, 'It's just for show, something I keep for protection. It's only got blanks in it. I wouldn't want to hurt anyone.'

I would, Bigeyes. The grunt for starters. And his mates. And a good few other nebs.

'I'd never fired it before that time in the bunga-low,' she says. 'But then I had to use it again—'

'Outside the warehouse.'

'Yes.'

It's falling into place, sort of. I remember the gun-shots when I was lying on the ground with my head sprung. I thought I'd been shot. But I was out of my brain by then. Out of my body, out of everything.

But there's still questions.

How did she find me? How did she know my name? She's not one of the dregs out looking for me, or the mean-crack gobbos who sent 'em, or any of the other grudgy scumbos who want a piece of me. But she's no muffin either.

I got to be careful with this one.

She's talking again, still low but faster, like she knows the nurse is coming back any second. I'm glad. I want to hear. I don't want to talk but I want to hear.

'The men ran out of the bungalow. I don't know where they went. But I knew I had to get out quick. They could come back any moment. They wouldn't be scared of an old woman for long. They'd regroup and come back.'

She's breathing fast now.

'I picked up Buffy and carried her out into the garden. There's a small tree at the bottom and some softer ground to the right of it. I dug a quick grave and put her in it, and covered it over. Then I got my things from the bungalow and hurried out.'

'Where to?'

'Doesn't matter.' Her voice sounds sharp for a moment. But it soon softens again. 'You don't need to know where I went. I was a bit confused anyway, at first. A bit scared.'

'But you phoned the police.'

'Not straightaway.'

She goes quiet again, in spite of the nurse coming

back. I want her to spew some more. There's loads I got to know. She didn't phone the porkers. Why not?

I already know, Bigeyes.

'You're on the run,' I say.

She doesn't answer.

'You are,' I say.

'You don't know that. You don't know anything about me.'

'I know that wasn't your bungalow.'

She looks away. I feel slightly guilty. She's helped me—more than once. She's probably even saved my life. I shouldn't push her. She hasn't got to tell me stuff. I'm not going to tell her stuff.

'Thanks,' I say.

She looks back at me. Her face is still dark but I can see the eyes moving. She doesn't believe me. Don't blame her. I wouldn't believe me if I was her.

'I mean it,' I say.

She doesn't answer. Just goes on looking. I prompt her.

'Can you tell me some more?'

She glances over her shoulder.

'She's not there yet,' I say.

I've been watching for the nurse too. Mary goes on checking, then turns back to me.

'I phoned the police,' she says. 'But I didn't do it that day. I was in too much of a state. I should have had the nerve. I might have saved that poor girl's life.'

I don't answer. I just wait. I want her to finish. I want her to say everything.

'I rang the next day,' she says. 'I didn't give the police my name. I'm not telling you why. I just described the men. By that time the news had broken about that girl's murder in the bungalow. What was her name? Trixi Kenton. And your description was going round.' She pauses. 'I didn't say I'd seen you.'

'OK.'

'Does that mean thank you?'

I don't answer. She waits a moment longer, then goes on.

'But I met this girl.'

It's got to be Bex.

'Down by the river,' she says.

'What did you go down there for?'

'Never mind. I had my reasons.' Mary pauses again. I catch a glint of green in her eyes. Then the darkness swallows it. 'I was there anyway. And I saw you down the path. You were staggering across it onto the waste ground and you were streaming blood. Then you headed for the old warehouse.'

I don't believe this, Bigeyes.

'And there were these men,' she says. 'I didn't know most of them, but I recognized the fat man and one of the others. They were following you towards the warehouse.'

I still don't believe this. There's no way an old woman would follow those gobbos. Not to try and rescue me.

'I was going to turn and find a policeman,' she goes on. 'I'd seen a couple further down the quay. But then this girl—'

'Bex.'

'She didn't give her name. She just climbed out of one of the old hulks by the riverside and came racing up to me. She was in a terrible state. Said we had to do something or those men would kill you. And she told me your name. She said you were called Blade.'

I close my eyes and listen on. And now I'm

stinging inside. Cos you know what, Bigeyes? I owe this old girl big time.

Again.

Cos she came on after me all by herself. Bex ran off, like she would, but the old girl came on, and found me with the gobbos, and pulled out that crazy gun again, and fired it.

Two gunshots.

One for each time she's saved my life.

The nurse is talking.

'Lily, that's enough. Let him rest now.'

Lily? Did you hear that, Bigeyes? The old girl's call-ing herself Lily. I don't believe it. And the nurse's drinking it up. She's something else, that Mary. Or whatever her name is.

I'm calling her Mary anyway. I told you once before—I don't give two bells about names. Mary speaks again, a whisper, dead close.

'Listen.' She's talking fast, confidential, so the nurse can't hear. 'I don't know why I'm saying this but . . . well, I'll say it anyway. I don't know who you are or what you've done. And I'm not asking. But I know you're in a heap of trouble.'

She hesitates, then hurries on.

'If you ever need to find me, ask for Jacob at The Crown in South Street. I can't promise to help you. But I can promise to listen. And you keep what I've just said to yourself, OK?'

'Lily.' The nurse again, all bossy. 'That's enough now.'

There's a silence. I wait for a bit, peek out the corner of an eye. Mary's gone but the nurse is still there. Sees me watching.

'You need to sleep,' she says. 'We can talk again when you've had some more rest.' A pause, then, 'But can you just tell me what your name is?'

I close the eye, act dozy. Nurse goes on.

'Only Lily didn't know and no one else does either.'

I don't answer.

'Is it Slicky?' she says. 'I mean, is that your nickname?'

I go on acting sleepy. Nurse doesn't speak again. I feel her tuck the sheets, linger for a bit, slip out. I keep my eyes closed, peer up at the lids. They feel heavy, like my thoughts.

I'm struggling, Bigeyes, struggling to think. But I got to. And I got to act. I just wish Mary had had longer. There's more I need to know. Though I can guess most of what happened outside the warehouse.

Mary fires the gun and clears out the gobbos. They wig it out of sight. Sound of the shots attracts the police. Mary puts the gun away before they turn up, says she didn't see anything, just heard the shots and found this boy lying wounded. Porkers call the ambulance and here I am. Mary comes with 'em.

No one's linked her and me. She's just some old bird who was on the spot at the time. That's why she's been allowed in to see me. Bex blasted off somewhere else. Like she would.

Who knows?

Whatever story Mary's told, they've bought it. Only now they're guessing I'm the boy called Slicky who's been on the news. So there'll be porkers in the hospital corridor waiting for me to come round.

And they're the nicest of the nebs I got to lose. I don't even want to think about the grinks waiting. They'll all know where I am now. How many of 'em are outside? And how many have slimed in?

I got to get out of here.

Wait a bit, listen cute, open my eyes, check round. Empty ward, lights off, except down the corridor. Sit up, check round again. Brain's swimming. I feel weak, dizzy, choked up. Head's pounding where Dig's knife fizzed me.

But I can think. I can feel. And what I feel is fear.

They're close, Bigeyes. They're all around us.

I got to do this, no matter what state I'm in. Pull back the sheet, edge my feet onto the floor, test my weight. Shit, I'm swaying. I'm standing but I got no balance. And I still got this effing drip in my arm.

Back on the bed, breathing hard, half-sitting, half-lying. I'm shaking like a dungpot. Got to get a grip. Got to think what to do. If I can't move, I'm drummed.

Footsteps.

Down the corridor.

Glance towards the door. No one there but some-one's close. It's not the nurse. I can tell. Check round the room. There's got to be something I can use as a weapon if I need one. Cos I'm telling you, Bigeyes, the nebs who want me won't fuss over a hospital. They want me too bad for that.

Footsteps getting louder. There's more than one person.

Two, maybe three.

No weapon, nothing I can use. Got to hope it's just staff. No other choice. Back into bed, pull the sheets over, close my eyes again, almost. Peep out. Watch the door.

Three gobbos looking in. They're not staff. I'm watching cute. Don't know if they've worked out I'm awake. But they're watching. They're standing there, looking in.

I don't know these guys. Don't think so anyway. Can't see 'em clear with the lights off. Could be OK. But I don't think so. They don't smell like muffins. They're not porkers either. I always know porkers.

Nurse's voice down the corridor.

'Can I help you?'

Gobbos turn round. Nurse speaks again.

'Can I help you?'

'We're looking for a friend,' says one.

Cool voice, cultured. This guy's slick.

'A patient?' says the nurse.

'Yes. Is this the Neurology Department?'

'You've gone past it. Back down the corridor, turn right at the end and keep going.'

'Thanks.'

Sound of footsteps tramping away. Then more, heading in my direction. Nurse's face appears in the doorway. I close my eyes right up, breathe slow. Footsteps up to the bed. Feel her check me over, fiddle with the sheets. Voice in the doorway, a gobbo.

'Jenny? Do you know who those men were?'

'No, doctor.' Nurse goes on tucking in the sheets. 'They said they were looking for a patient in the Neurology Department.'

'Did you believe them?'

'No.'

Neither did I, Bigeyes. They're grinks. And they'll be back.

Silence. I keep my eyes closed, listen, think. I can sense the doctor's still in the doorway. Nurse stops fiddling. But they're watching me dead cute, both of 'em. I can feel it. Keep my breathing steady. Got to sound asleep.

Then wig it out of here soon as they're gone.

Doctor speaks again.

'I'll ask staff to keep their eyes open. We can't have unauthorized people wandering about. How is he?'

'Not sure. I think he might have tried to get out of bed. The sheets were a bit of a mess when I came in just now. But maybe he just twisted in his sleep.'

More footsteps drawing close. Got to be the doc. I can feel 'em still watching me. Doc speaks.

'Well, he won't get very far if he does try to get out of bed. Not with an injury like that and the amount of blood he's lost. He'll do himself serious harm if he tries to move. Let's hope he's sensible and doesn't do anything stupid.'

Yeah, right, doc. You've worked out I'm maybe not sleeping. Got your message. But it makes no difference. When you and Nursey are gone, I'm gone too.

Sound of footsteps, his and hers, back to the door, then they stop. No more sounds. Keep my eyes well closed. They're still there by the door, watching. Doc's no fleabrain. I can tell. And Nursey's nobody's dimp.

Trouble is, I got to be even more careful now. The porkers will already have told the staff to keep an eye on me. And now these two have worked out I tried to get out of bed. They'll be watching more cute than ever.

That's going to make it harder for me to get out. And it won't be enough to stop the grinks. Those three gobbos might not come back. But somebody else will. I got to wig it out of here—somehow.

Only I can't yet. I got to play stealth first. Got to wait a bit. Still no sound of footsteps from the door. Doc and nurse are still watching. Keep my breathing steady, my eyes closed. I can see Mary's face inside the lids. And Buffy's too. I'm sorry she got killed. She was one crazy dog, but I liked her.

And I've got that grunt on my list.

Footsteps at last. They're moving off down the corridor. It's a good sound. But I'm keeping my eyes closed a bit longer to be safe. Got to make sure they've really gone. Couple of minutes. Couple more. Should be OK now.

Ease up the lids.

'So you're awake,' says a voice.

A hand splats over my mouth, a knife pricks at my

throat. It's one of those gobbos, the one who spoke to the nurse.

Keep still. Nothing I can do. He's too strong and I'm too weak. He's going to rub me out or he's going to take me. One or the other. Can't stop either right now. So keep still.

Got to act like I'm blown out, like I'm no trouble. He might just hesitate and give me a slot. Keep my lids low, peer up. I can see the shape of him, just. No sign of the other two.

He leans down. He's wearing a doc's coat. Keep my eyes glazed. Make like I'm drugged, like I'm stumpy in the head. I might just get a chance to do something.

But there'll only be one slam.

Got to act like I got nothing in me. Then hit when I can.

His eyes are close to mine. He's drilling me, peering in. Roll my eyes, let 'em mist up. But I got a good shot of him now. Tall gobbo, thirty odd, ice cold. Never seen him before today.

The knife's moving, stroking my throat.

He likes this. He's having fun. I stay glazed, go on

acting limp. He keeps his other hand tight over my mouth, leans closer, whispers.

'Time to get you out of here.'

And then he moves, fast. Hands flip back but before I can make a sound, he's got tape squeaked over my lips and round my cheeks. Next moment he's ripped the needle and drip out of my arm, and the knife's back over my throat.

He's chill, this gobbo. And he's a pro.

He checks the doorway. Nobody there, no sounds in the corridor. He looks back, gives a little grin. Strokes the blade over my skin, grabs me by the hair, eases my head up from the bed.

'No point acting,' he murmurs. 'You're wide awake.'

I keep my eyes glazed. Got to keep doing it, whatever he says. Got to make like I'm spaced. Got to bide my time, keep my strength, wait for the moment, take him by surprise. And it won't be easy. He's no dum-flush dreg like Paddy's gobbos.

He sits me up, his eyes close to mine again. I can feel him peering hard. He's searching inside my head, trying to click onto me. I stay glazed, limp.

Feel a sudden shock.

My body jerks forward. Can't help it. I know what he's done. He's dinked me with the knife. Just a little one at the base of the spine to shake me up. And now he's peering inside my head again. Keep glazed, keep limp. Hang down in his arms.

He's not bluffed. He knows I'm playing dog-eye with him.

'Won't work,' he whispers.

Another dink of the knife. I jerk forward again, into his arms. He pulls my head in close to his, and there's his eyes searching my skull again. Somehow I keep glazing back. He's getting impatient now. Or maybe he's starting to wonder a bit. Got to hope he is. Got to make him feel I'm no sweat. Got to squeeze a lapse out of him.

He straightens up suddenly, pulls me by the hair towards the edge of the bed, gets his arms round my legs and twists them so I'm sitting there, slopped over.

'Put these on,' he mutters.

He's found some clothes. Or brought 'em.

'They should fit you,' he says.

I slump back on the bed.

'Sit up.' He's getting angry now. 'Or I'll make you.'

I don't move.

He yanks me upright again, his eyes dark. Whips the knife in front of my face, flints it from side to side, trying to make my eyes follow. Blade glints but I keep glazed.

Suddenly he flings me back on the bed. He's crouched over me, dead close, too close. I try to open my mouth. It's no good. Tape's on too tight. And now he's pulling off my hospital gown.

I hate this. I got pictures from the past flashing by. I want to squirm, fight back. But I got to go on playing dog-eye. Got to stay limp, stay like I don't know what's going on.

He's got the gown off me now. I'm naked on the bed, gobbo bent over me, knees either side of my body. And he's touching me again. Only thank Christ, not that other way.

But it's still bad.

He's pulling the shirt on me, and then the sweater, and the pants and trousers, and socks and shoes. He's quick and clever, and suddenly I'm dressed and he's looking round at the door.

Still nobody there.

He's off the bed now, picking me up.

'Time to go,' he mouths.

And he's carrying me towards the door.

I stay limp, let my arms hang loose. He doesn't bother about them. Feels confident he can handle me. And he can right now. I feel like I got no strength at all. I'm just hoping I can find enough to do the business if I get a chance.

And I got to make a chance.

Cos once he's got me outside the hospital, it's over.

He won't be working alone. I told you. There's lots of grinks after me. There's the ones who want to rub me out for what I did. The enemies of my enemies. And there's the ones who want me alive. But that's only so they can torture me for what they want to know. And when they got that, they'll rub me out too.

So either way, it's bad.

I got to do something, got to make a chance, got to find something in me to nail this guy. He's stopped at the door, checking round. Nobody in the corridor. He sets off down it, carrying me easy. I'm lolling in his arms now. But I'm thinking quick.

He can't take me out the main entrance. He's got to find a side way out. Maybe the way he trigged in. Question is: which way's he going? I never been inside this hospital till now. But I know the streets round it.

I know 'em good, Bigeyes. Like I know all the city.

I'm trying to think. Which way would I go if I had to sneak out of here? I already know the answer. But he's got a different agenda. He's going to meet his mates. He stops near the end of the corridor.

Voices further down, round the corner. Move my hand a little, loose and swingy. Want to see if I can work it closer to his knife. He's still got it in his hand. I can feel the flat of the blade against my body as he keeps me close.

He senses the movement and I let my arm flop again. He looks round at me, gives a little knowing smile, turns back towards the sound of the voices, then opens a door to the left.

Don't remember seeing this, but it's no surprise. I was blacko when I came in here. He carries me through the door, shuts it behind us, dead quiet. We're in another corridor. Moves down it to the end, turns right. Halfway down, another door.

He pulls out a key, slots it in, opens the door. Little storeroom with mops, pails, cleaning stuff. Bottles of this and that. White coats hanging on hooks.

And a dead body lying on the floor.

Middle-aged gobbo, one of the cleaners maybe. Scumbo probably just wanted one of the white coats. Saw the gobbo inside the room, strangled him, changed coats, nicked the key. And now he wants to slip back into his old coat and stroll out of here like nothing's happened.

There you go—his own coat at the back. He's shoved one of those giant refuse bags on top. And I know why. He's going to stuff me inside it, so he doesn't look like he's carrying some kid. I'm thinking fast. It's got to be now. I got to wipe this guy in here.

Yeah, Bigeyes, I got to kill him. No other way. It's him or me. And I can't screw up like I did with Paddy. I got to do the business, just like I used to. Got to find what I once had and settle this thing. Or we're done. Trust me, we're done.

Good news is he's got to put me down to change his coat. Bad news is I hardly got any strength. It's like I said, Bigeyes—one slam. That's all I'm going to get.

If that.

He closes the door behind us, slips the key in the lock, turns it. He's holding me close again, peering into my eyes like before. He's trying one last time to fix me. But he can't get inside my head. I'm still playing dog-eye.

He's even more dangerous like this. Part of him's decided I'm too weak to hurt him. But part of him's wary. Which part's stronger? That's the crack of it. If it's the first, I still got a chance for that one slam.

If it's the other, he'll glue his eyes on me too tight.

He stiffens. He's made up his mind.

Stay limp, stay focused, stay ready. He's moving, slow, his left arm under my legs, the other clammed round my body. Knife's in his right hand, brushing my arm.

Stay still. Wait.

He bends down, slow, slow. He's watching me

cute. I can feel his eyes burning me, even with mine half-closed. Floor's coming closer. It's touching my feet, legs, bum, back, head.

He lets go. I flop back, roll my arms to the side, loll my head. He stands over me like a shadow. He's looking down. I can feel it. He wants to kill me so much. I can feel that too. He doesn't want to keep me alive, take me back. He likes killing. I know it.

He's found me, he's got me. That's trophy number one. Trophy number two will be bringing me in. But he doesn't want that. Too much trouble. And not enough fun. He wants trophy number three.

Taking me out.

But he's not allowed. He's been told he's got to bring me in. So he's looking down right now, and he's hating me for that. For all his cool, he's boiling inside. He moves, just a little, his right leg lifting over me. He's stepping off, reaching for the shelf.

Rustle of coats changing. The crackle of the refuse bag. The right leg moving back where it was. He's standing over me again, looking down. I don't need to see him to know that. I can feel everything I need to feel right here, on the floor, eyes closed.

I can feel him watching, shifting his weight from foot to foot, checking me over, checking I'm safe. Another rustle of the bag. He's bending down. He's drawing close. He stops. He's thinking how to do this. Pick the kid up and drop him in the bag or bend down further and roll him into it?

Wait, listen. Get ready.

He's moving again, bending close. He's going to pick me up first. Another rustle as he lets go the bag. Left hand slips under my legs again. Right's still got the knife. I can feel the blade as he slides his hand over my arm.

I'm moving up again, closer, closer, closer to his head.

And then I turn.

Sharp.

My right hand thrusting for his face.

He's not ready. He doesn't catch my arm. I'm through his guard and his eyes have pricked wide. And that's good. They're my target.

I stab 'em with the only blades I got.

My fingers.

One in each eye.

Hard.

He gives a yell, flicks his head back, slaps his left hand over his face. But I'm on his right wrist now. I've got his little finger in one hand, thumb in the other. I jerk both ways.

Snap!

Snap!

He roars and lunges, but I'm too good at this. I got the knife, I'm on his back and the blade's moving over his throat.

But then it stops.

I've frozen—again. I'm clinging to him, his hair tight in the squeeze of my hand, the knife in my other hard against his throat. A red drip's trickling down his neck.

It should be a river by now.

He should be on the floor, his eyes dimming up, his sick life pumping over his chest. But he's still standing. He's moaning from his broken finger and thumb, and he's trembling, sweating, waiting for the moment. He thinks I'm taking my time, making him squirm before I wipe him out.

He knows what I can do. He doesn't know I've lost it.

Not yet.

When he works that out, I'm dead.

He's still waiting. But he's picked something up. I can sense it. I can feel his mind starting to move, starting to hope. I got to snuff that out. Got to bluff things, play strong. Even if I can't kill him, I got to make out I can.

And find some other way out of this.

He speaks.

'Thought I'd be dead by now.'

Low voice, checking me out. I stroke the blade over his throat. He stiffens, but not enough. He's not as scared as he was.

'Don't tell me you're losing it, boy.'

Defiance in his voice now. I lock my legs round him, let go of his hair, rip the tape off my mouth, grab his hair again, jerk his head back.

'Ah!' he goes.

I push the blade hard against his throat. Another red drip trickles down his neck. I wait till he feels it, lean close to his ear.

'What's my name, Scumbo?'

He doesn't answer. He's panting, his eyes flicking at me.

'I said what's my name?'

'Blade,' he breathes.

'Say it again.'

'Blade.'

'Louder.'

'Blade, Blade, Blade.'

'Carry me to the door.'

He steps past the other guy's body, stops at the door.

'Turn round.'

He turns, facing back into the room. I keep the knife hard against his throat. He's still not scared enough. I can feel him starting to crack me. He's working out why he's not dead. I got to move quick before he tries something.

'Down on your knees.'

He doesn't move. He's testing me again. Got to act now or he'll have me.

Rasp the knife over his throat, scrape some of the blood onto the blade, hold it in front of his eyes so he can see it. He stiffens again, his eyes fixed on the knife. Whip it back to his throat.

'I said down on your knees.'

He drops to his knees, my legs still straddling him, the knife against his throat. I let go of his hair, reach back with my free hand, unlock the door, pull out the key.

'Lost the bottle, have you?' he says suddenly. 'To kill me?'

There's mockery in his voice now. I lean close again.

'Kill you?' I run the blade up and down his neck. 'Is that what you want, big man?'

He doesn't answer. I whisper into his ear.

'Put your hands behind your back.'

He doesn't move. He's stiffened again, sweat pouring like before.

'You might regret that last remark, Scummy.'

'Listen—'

'Put your hands behind your back.'

He moves his hands slowly behind him. He's trembling again, but so am I now. I got to do this real quick. I jump off and kick him hard in the back. He falls forward and his face thuds against the floor. I slip out of the room, slam the door after me and lock it. From inside comes Scumbo's voice.

Hard, dangerous.

'You're dead, kid. You know that? Cos you've lost it. You couldn't kill Paddy. You couldn't kill me. You're finished. And you know it.'

The door starts pounding and a crack appears round the lock.

Down the corridor, quick as I can. Got to get out of here somehow. Problem is, all the strength I had went into nailing that gobbo. Don't know what I got left except fear. But maybe that's enough to shift me.

Least there's nobody here and no sound of voices or footsteps, just the pounding of the door behind him. He'll be out of there any second. End of the corridor, through the exit.

Two more corridors, right and left. Three nurses halfway down one of 'em. Haven't seen me yet. Nobody in the other. Slip down that, stop at the door, check through the glass panel.

Another corridor, also empty.

Hope it stays like this. Cos you know what, Bigeyes? There is a way out of here. If I can just stay lucky and find the grit. I know what's waiting for me outside. Not just those two gobbos I saw with Scumbo.

There's all the others.

I'll never make it out any of the normal exits. Not in this state. Not even if I was crack-hot. All the exits'll be watched. But there's another way out if I can just get there. And if I can find my way back into the city, she'll take care of me. I got a snug not far away. Not one of the best but it'll do. If I can just get there, I can rest. And think.

But first we got to get out of the hospital.

Into the next corridor. I'm moving slow now. Every step feels tough and my head-wound's hurting. Got to keep going. Still nobody here but I'm listening hard, watching cute. Drone of cars outside the hospital. Window ahead.

Slow down, ease close. Don't want anyone to see me from outside. Stop, peep through. Car park below. Dark, very dark. That's good and bad. Good cos they can't see me so easy. Bad cos I can't see them.

Well, I can a bit. Enough lights to spot some of the nebs. Most of 'em are muffins. I can tell. Just people

coming and going. I'm looking for the grinks. The ones
not moving. They'll be out there. They'll be trying to
look like muffins. But I'll know 'em.

There's one.

Over by the far end of the car park. Check him out,
Bigeyes. See the ticket machine? Left of that. Got him?
Gobbo in a long coat, lighting a cig. Standing by the
Citroën. Looks like he's waiting for a friend. Only he's
not.

He's waiting for me.

Another one further to the right. Close to the
ambulance bay. Tall gobbo, shiny forehead. Kind of guy
who looks like he'd help anyone. Well, he wouldn't
help me.

Come on. We can't hang about here.

Back from the window, crouch, creep past, on
down the corridor. End's getting closer. Got to watch
it. No door this time, just another corridor cutting past.
And Scumbo's mates could be waiting round the other
side.

Draw close. No sound of anything round the corner of the wall. No feeling of anyone. I usually know. I
don't need to hear. I can feel if someone's there. Only

that's when I'm strung right. I'm lugged in the brain right now, not thinking good. That's when I make mistakes. I got to watch extra cute or I'll crash my gut.

Stop at the corner of the wall.

Listen again. Nothing. Wait, try to feel what's round there. Why can't I do it? I used to feel, used to know. But I'm hurt too bad. Body's messed up, head's messed up. I'm trembling again.

Stick my head round the corner.

It's a risk but I'm desperate. And I'm lucky again.

No one there. Just another empty corridor. Door at the end, lift to the right, emergency exit to the left. That's probably the way Scumbo was going to take me. Out the emergency exit and into the car park.

His mates'll be close by, most likely just outside. I got to be careful now. If they see me, I'm done. Trouble is, to do what I want, I got to get down to the end of that corridor.

Move. Make yourself do it.

Down the corridor, slow. Ease myself close to the wall.

Here's the emergency exit. Just praying nobody's on the other side. They can't get in that way. But I'm still in trouble if they spot me.

Only chance I got to wig it is if no one sees me.

And that's asking a lot.

Least the corridor's still quiet. Here's the exit. I'm still hidden from the outside. But not for much longer. Creep forward, inch at a time. Glass panel's in view. I can see the darkness outside and one tiny corner of the car park beyond.

No sign of any figures from here.

But I'm not up to the panel yet. I'm at an angle. I'm still trembling and the pain in my head's growing worse.

Reach up, touch my brow. Feels sticky. It's bleeding. I can feel it. That didn't come from fighting Scumbo.

That's my wound loosening up.

Another step towards the panel, another, peep round, holding my breath. No one there. No one close anyway. But I can see the two gobbos further down. Got 'em? One behind the Renault, one over to the right, behind the van.

Looking this way.

Just hope they haven't seen me here. They haven't moved. I think they're too far back to see clear. And the corridor's a bit dark. Even so, I got to be even more careful with the next bit. Look to the right.

You got it, Bigeyes. We're taking the lift.

Crouch right down, cheek against the floor. And now crawl. Even this is risky. I'm still visible through the emergency exit. And it's not just Scumbo's two mates I'm worried about. It's all the other grinks out there.

But I got no choice.

I got to crawl and hope.

Reach up, press the button for the lift. I'm praying there'll be no one in it. Whirring sound, chink of a bell, clunk of the doors opening. I'm still lying here, hoping.

It's empty. Roll into the lift, crawl to the side, out of the sight-line from the emergency exit. Stand up, swaying. Spot of blood nicks the floor. Check my pockets. No handkerchief. Reach up, press my sleeve against the wound, hold it there, take it away. Cuff's all red.

But I can't be doing with that now.

Reach out, press the button.

Top floor.

Doors close. Judder of the lift as it moves. We're going up. I'm tracking the floors. Third, fourth, fifth, sixth. Praying no one'll get on. Lift stops.

Sixth floor.

Shit, there's three more to go.

Turn my back on the doors, kneel down like I'm doing my laces. Hear the doors open, woman's voice out in the corridor.

'Can you help me?'

I don't look round.

'I said can you help me?'

Bit of a stewpot. I don't want to look at her. Voice comes again, angry now.

'Are you deaf or something?'

Then a gobbo's voice.

'Mrs Baker, you're not supposed to be out here on your own.'

I hear the doors closing again. Glance round. Old

woman in a wheelchair, glaring in at me. Male nurse fussing over her.

'Mrs Baker—'

'I want to go in the lift.'

'Mrs—'

But the doors have closed and we're moving on. Only down again. Christ, Bigeyes, this is sticking me in. It wouldn't be so bad if I was strong. But I feel so weak, so useless. It's not just my body. It's my mind. I feel split inside.

I want to scream so bad.

And now the lift's taking me back down.

Stops again. Third floor. This time I don't kneel down. This time I got to do something else. Doors open. Ancient gobbo standing there on his own, waiting to get in. Only I'm blocking the way.

'All right, Grandpa?' I give him a manic grin. 'Coming in to join me, are you?'

He stares. Not sure what to do.

'Take you up or take you down, Gramps?' I give him a wink. 'Make it down, Claphead. That's where I'm going.'

He takes a step back. I press the button.

'See you around, Gramps.'

Doors close. And the lift starts to climb again.

Yeah, I know. Risky. But what else can I do? Can't hang around any longer. And I can't have anyone in the lift. All I can do is hope the old boy'll keep quiet about it. And if he reports it, he might just say I was going down, not up.

They're going to see I'm gone anyway soon. They probably know already. There's no time to lose. Lift's moving good. Keep going, keep going. Don't stop. It doesn't stop. It's moving, up, up, up. Three floors to go, two floors, one.

Ding!

Top floor. Doors open. Nobody out there, thank Christ. Hum of talk somewhere round to the left. Creep out. Doors close behind my back. Whirr of the lift as it heads back down. Look right and left.

No wards up here, like I hoped. Never been here before. But I know what I want. It's not a choice I wanted to make, not being so weak. But it's the only one left. And if I'm going to die, I don't want it to be the grinks that get me, you know what I mean?

But I'm not dead yet, Bigeyes.

There's still a chance. If I can just find the strength.

Check round. Voices still coming from the left. Gobbos talking. No sign of anyone but a half-open door at the end of the corridor. That's fine, whoever you are, long as you stay in there. Creep round to the right. Narrow corridor, offices and stuff.

Where's the bit I want?

There.

Staff Only.

Door to the outside. Little twist of steps climbing up. Another emergency exit. Check round. Still no sign of anyone. That's one bit of good news. Thought I'd have to duck and slink. Over to the door, check round again.

Nobody.

Press the bar, open the door, close it behind me, up to the roof. Wind blams me like a fist. Christ, Bigeyes, it's freezing up here. Head's swimming with pain now. I can't stay long up here. I got to move quick. There's nothing to be gained by hanging around.

OK—two ways out. One bad, one worse.

But before we decide, we got to check things out. Now listen up, Bigeyes—I'm going to tell you something. That's right, another thing I haven't told you. Get over it. I said I've never been in the hospital before. That was true. But one thing I didn't tell you.

I've been on it.

That's right. I've been up here. Roof's a good place if it's warm and you got to keep out of sight. I used to come up here a lot when I first hit the city. Before I found my snugs.

Haven't come up for a good while. Haven't needed to. Got enough places to chill. But this was a good one in the beginning. And there's lots of other roofs to use. It's like a city of its own up here. And it's safer than down on the streets.

Once you know it, you can move easy. Cos I'll tell you something else—I can't run good, but I can climb good. And I know how to get off this place. Two ways, like I said.

One would be a whack if I was well. But I'm not so it's bad. More than bad—it's lethal. As for the other way, well, let's check it out. But I already know what I'm going to see.

Come on, Bigeyes. Let me show you how many friends I haven't got. Over to the edge, crouch down, crane over. Check it out. What do you see down there?

Nothing?

Look again. I know it's dark but look, keep looking. Go on—what do you see? Still nothing? You blind or something? There, far left. See the street running off the car park? That's Whiteacre Lane. How many figures do you see?

Christ, Bigeyes, you must be looking out your stump. Or maybe I'm just more used to this. I've been used to it all my life. Looking and finding. Knowing where the shit lives.

There, end of the street—one figure. Another one in Belton Avenue. Another one further up. Another one round the corner of Nelson Drive. There'll be more in some of those cars.

Yeah, I know. You're thinking they're just figures, just nebs. Harmless little muffins living their muffiny lives. They're not, Bigeyes. They're grinks. I always know. And I haven't finished yet. Move on, round the side of the roof. Keep checking down.

See 'em? More round this side of the building. Move on. More again. Count 'em. How many have you seen? I've seen twelve. And there'll be others. I'm guessing twenty plus round the hospital. And there'll be more in the streets round about, case I get through the first crunch.

Don't shake your head.

They're grinks. They're from the past.

And they've come back.

That's why we can't use the exits. That's why we can't take the emergency steps down. So there's only one way left. As I expected.

Let's get it over with.

Back end of the roof, away from the main entrance. Creep up to the edge. Check over. What do you see from this side?

Yeah, yeah, more buildings. That's just hospital stuff. What else? Playing fields beyond, OK. I'm not talking about them. Closer in. Check over the edge. Right over. Follow the wall down. What do you see?

More emergency steps.

That's how I used to get up here. Only we can't take 'em. Not all the way down. Too risky. There's grinks watching this part of the complex too. But we can take the steps a little way down. It might just be too high up for those dungpots on the ground to see us in the dark.

Got to try anyway.

Let's go.

Over the edge, foot on the step, another, then down. Wind's butting me bad now. I'm shivering, my head's still swimming and the pain's getting worse. My wound's shedding blood again. Can't stop to fiddle with it. Got to hold on, and this is the easy bit.

Twenty foot down, twenty-five, thirty.

Stop.

Now it gets nasty. Look left, Bigeyes, straight along the wall. That's right, a ledge. Yeah, I know. More a mantelpiece than a ledge, but it's strong. I know cos I've been on it before.

And it's all we got now.

Grip the rail, ease one foot off the steps onto the ledge, then the other. Let go the rail. Shit, Bigeyes, this is worse than I remember. It was bad enough when I wasn't bombed. I got my balance skimming loose again, and the wind's swirling worse than ever.

Stay still, dead still, breathe. Nothing to hold on to

now. Just the flat wall against me and nothing to grip. Keep my face to the wall, take another breath, inch myself along, step, step, step. Got to reach the far edge. Got to just . . . reach the far edge.

Step, step, step.

Wind's getting worse. Colder, stronger. I want to look down, check if there's grinks watching. But I can't. I got my face close against the wall. And I don't dare shift it.

Step, step, step.

Edge of the wall's getting closer. Another ten steps and I'm there. If I can just keep upright, not buck out. Cos I want to. I'm telling you, Bigeyes, I'm close to losing my drift.

Here's the edge.

And here's the next jip. Cos it's not over yet, Bigeyes. That was the fun bit just gone. Gets worse now. Up to the edge, hand round, arm round, inch past onto the other wall. And now, check again. What do you see?

Ledge continues along this wall. And further along?

Drainpipe cutting through it, up and down. That's right, Bigeyes. We got to reach that. And then we got to climb down. And then . . .

Follow the pipe with your eyes.

Thirty foot down, forty maybe—little guttery thing in the wall. See it? Kind of like a stone basin. Don't ask me what it does. But that's where we put our feet, that's where we launch off. Where to?

Look left. Look down.

Yeah, Bigeyes. Told you this was a whack. We got to jump down onto the top of the Grosvenor Hotel. Don't ask me how far it is. I don't want to think about it. Enough to break a few bones if you hit the roof badly.

But the alternative's a lot worse.

And it is jumpable. There's kids do this kind of thing all the time. I used to be good at it. And this jump's a jink if you know how to do it. If you're into jumping over roofs. Which I was. When I was strong. And desperate.

Only now I'm not strong.

I'm just desperate.

So I guess it's jump and hope. A chance of safety if I make it. A three or four second drop if I don't. Just long enough to say goodbye to sweet Becky before the ground splats out my life.

Let's go.

Down the ledge, steady. Keep up, Bigeyes. Don't dawdle. I'm not doing this on my own. Keep moving. It's when you stop that you freeze in your head. And then you're stuffed. Got to keep moving, keep thinking it's possible.

Cos it is.

I keep telling myself it is. I know I'm blasted. Body's smashed, mind's smashed. But I got to keep telling myself I can do it. I found something to nail that scumbo. Something fear gave me. I need that again.

I need it now.

Or in a couple of short minutes. When I'm standing on that stony lip. I got to find that thing again. The strength, nerve, luck—whatever it is fear grubbed into me last time. I need it back. I need fear to deliver.

Here's the drainpipe. Got to watch things big time now. Got to hang on good. It's not about standing any more. That was hard enough. But I need strength for this. Got to grip that thing tight. If it slips out of my arms, I'm falling.

And it's over.

Ease round, one leg, slow. Test the foot against the side, dig the toe in behind the pipe, lock it against the wall. Feels cute but I haven't put any weight on it yet. Breathe, breathe again. I don't like this, Bigeyes. I don't feel safe.

But I got to do it.

Arm round the pipe, tight as I can, ease my body round. I'm clinging on now and I can feel my weight pulling me back. Cling on, tighter, tighter. I'm still there. I haven't fallen. Not yet.

Ease down, other foot digging round the pipe into the wall, then the first foot again, arms still tight. I feel like a baby clutching its mum. And just as weak. But I'm moving down, foot by foot.

Twist my head, check below. I can see the basin-thing. Beyond it the sheer drop. And beyond that, a jump away, the flat roof of the Grosvenor Hotel. Move on, down, down. Mustn't hurry. Got to keep my head. Keep my head and I keep my life.

Or my hope anyway.

Yeah, I'll settle for hope.

Here's the stony lip. Rest my foot on it, arms still locked round the drainpipe. I don't want to let the thing go but I got to. I got to make myself turn, face the drop, face the roof. Breathe, breathe again, turn.

Slow.

Let go one hand. Got to or I can't turn. Right arm's still clutching the pipe, left arm's free. I'm half-round now, checking my footing on the lip. It's wet and slippery where water from the drain's splattered over it. But I got to trust it. The lip's all I got to stand on now.

And somehow I got to let go my right arm.

Ease it free from the pipe, turn right round. Both arms behind me now, hands clasping the pipe. I never felt so naked in my life. And I've felt naked many times, Bigeyes. You better believe it.

But now's not the time to talk about that.

Now I got to jump.

Only I can't. I'm rigid. I'm stuck on the edge of a wall, looking down at the ground far below me. Only it's so dark I can hardly see it. There's no lights below. It's the side of the hospital. A lane where the delivery vans come in.

But I can't see 'em. Can't see any figures either.

Maybe there's grinks there. Maybe not. I've stopped caring. Cos there's only one thing left now.

One way to go. Peer over at the roof of the hotel. Did it always look so far away? I used to jump this for fun.

But it's a long time since I did anything for fun.

Goodbye, Bigeyes.

Another darkness, another death.

Another question. What is this place? Cos you know what? I've stopped knowing what lives, what dies. Stopped caring, almost. All that's certain is darkness. And the sound of sirens. And then I get it.

Death's tricked me yet again. Some gobbo, that Death. I hate him. But I'm coming to respect him. And I'll tell you what—he's a trickster. It's all sleight of hand with him. Not with others. The gobbo in the storeroom's dead. No messing. He's not coming back. Same as sweet Becky's dead. And don't ask me how many others.

But me? Me and Death? He's playing with me. He's having a giggle. He likes me not knowing. He leaves me with darkness. And questions. And the sound of sirens again. And then I know.

I'm alive. I'm lying somewhere. The roof of the

hotel, that's it. I've been blacko again. But now I'm awake, I'm aching all over, shivering, moaning, weeping stupid little tears out of my stupid little eyes.

And somewhere below I can hear 'em. The wailing of sirens. I know what that means. They've found the gobbo's body. They've found I've gone. Question is: who knows where I am now?

Are you there, Bigeyes? Cos I can't see you. Maybe you've gone. I got my eyes open, haven't I? Shit, they're closed.

Open my eyes. Still dark. Night's fallen over me like a cold kiss. But I can see the sky clear and good. I'm lying on my back, and I'm shivering and crying, and my body's hurting, and I'm looking up at the sky.

And there's stars out.

And a moon. A big, bright, funnyface moon.

God, it's beautiful.

Where are you, Bigeyes? I still can't see you. But it doesn't matter. I can see the moon and the stars. And they're better looking than you are anyway. But now I got you again. You're still there. Like a smelly shirt.

Always clinging on.

Don't know if I'm pleased. Don't know what I think.

Just know I can't stay here watching the sky. If I stay here, there'll be no question-marks with Death. No sleight of hand. He'll fold me up and put me in his little bag. But I'll tell you something, Bigeyes. If I had to go tonight, I'd like to go like this.

Looking at the stars. And the funnyface moon.

But I'm not ready to go yet.

I got to move my stump. You too, Bigeyes. We're getting out of here. I made it to the roof. I can't give up now. Not while we still got a chance. But first things first. Check for injuries.

Nothing. Must have landed smart. Don't remember it. Don't remember the jump or the landing. Must have been instinct did it. Don't remember hitting anything bad either. The blacko must have come from exhaustion.

Question is: how much more have I got left?

Roll over onto my side. Aching everywhere but no breaks, not even a sprain. Get up. Get yourself up. Make yourself do it. Up, swaying again. Head's like a fog but the cold's helping like it did before. Got to watch myself, got to keep thinking. Got to keep low. There's grinks all round the streets and the porkers coming will have scattered 'em further about.

There's no way out of any of the hotel exits. Too close to the hospital. I got to roof-hop a bit more. Just as well the jumps are easier from here. And just as well I know my way. I might even get a good whip on my first plan.

The snug. There's one near here. I told you. If I can just get there without the grinks or porkers clogging me, I can rest up, sort my head, blast out of the city.

Cos there's no staying here now, Bigeyes. City's over for me. She's been good to me. But stay much longer and she'll turn into my grave. I got to get away, somewhere safe, if I can find it. Or if I can't, then . . .

Back to the Beast. Yeah, the Big Beast.

Did I ever tell you about him?

Don't suppose I did. Cos I don't like talking about him. He's a place, Bigeyes. Huge great place. Bigger than the city, way bigger. And he's no gentleman. Least the city's a lady some of the time. The Beast's a gentleman none of the time.

You don't want to know him.

And neither do I. But I'm starting to wonder, you know? If I can't find somewhere else to hide, maybe I just got to go back. I don't want to. The Beast's the last place on earth I want to go.

It's where they first got me. Where they won't be expecting me. Maybe I could take the fight to them. But I'm talking grime now. First I got to stay alive. Got to get through the next five minutes.

The Beast can wait. I'll think about him another time.

On, over the roof, heading east. Keep to the middle. Hotel's a beauty for keeping out of sight. At this point anyway. Only place higher is the hospital and I'm hoping no neb's looking down from the upper floors.

Can't do much about that now anyway. Any luck and there'll be too much fuss over the dead body. But there'll be a police block round this part of the city soon enough. They'll know I can't get far.

So I got to get out quick as I can.

End of the hotel roof. Now the fun starts again. Down the pipe, easy jump to the roof of the bank. Over the tiles, keeping back from the street. On to the edge of the roof, drainpipe down to the next level, another easy jump to the library, and now it stays cute for a bit.

Buildings close together, almost like a terrace. I'm hoping one of the windows'll let me in so I can creep back down to the ground. There's one I know always used to be open. Dodgy catch and rotten timber. It's at the end of the row too. Best place to get out of here.

Clamber on. I'm hurrying now and I got to watch it. Hands and legs are sort of working but they're still not right. They're not feeling their way like they should. Head's still bad, and I'm fighting blacko again. I just want to get warm and curl up.

Even if it means I never wake again.

I got to fight that. I got to want life more than death.

Another roof gone, another, another. Sirens still screaming in the streets. How many porkers have gone past now? I don't know. They're all heading for the hospital. And I'm pushing hard the other way.

If I can just get down to the street, it's five minutes to my snug.

Another roof gone, and another, and here it is. The pizzeria. Only the pizzeria bit's lower down. Top part of the building's offices and storerooms and stuff. No one's ever there this time of night. I'm just hoping nobody's fixed that old window.

If the same nebs are still running the place, we might be lucky.

Over the tiles, round the far side, keep low. Down the drainpipe to the lower roof, along the flat, round the side, down the next pipe. Got to be slickeye now. We're much closer to the street. Just a side lane underneath us but there's nebs wandering up and down.

And they're twitchy now the porkers have started whopping their sirens.

But here's the window.

And yeah, you beauty—just as rotten as ever. Cling to the drainpipe, check the thing over. Voices from the lane below. Two waiters from the pizzeria, having a cig. Can't move till they're gone. They might hear me shift the window.

Another siren from the street. Gobbos head back to look.

Yank the window, flick the catch. Window opens and I'm in. Close it after me, slip through the room and out to the landing. I know where this leads. I slapped it rough here one time, sleeping among the boxes in one of the storerooms when it got too cold to kip on the roof. Same old landing. Same old stairs.

And I don't have to go near the pizza restaurant.

I can use the back door.

Down the stairs, slow, quiet. Head's still hurting and I'm desperate to lie down. But I can smell my escape. And my little snug just minutes away. Down to the ground floor, wait in the shadows by the entrance to the cellar. Sound of voices in the kitchen. Further on the clamour of the restaurant.

Turn from them, past the cellar, out the back door and into the yard. More sirens scream past in the street beyond. But this gate opens onto the lane. Check round it. Dark, empty. No porkers, no grinks.

Nobody.

I'm gone.

End of the lane, check round, over the road, down the alleyway. Check again. End of the alleyway, check again.

And again.

I don't trust my eyes. They're not working right. Nothing's working right. Brain's bombed. Got to think somehow. Got to make myself. Just a little way to go. But I got to get in there without some neb clapping my shadow.

Check down the alleyway again.

No sign of anyone following. Means nothing. You don't see the clever ones most of the time. But you can feel 'em if you're snagged up cute. Trouble is I'm not. Not now. I don't trust myself. I don't trust any part of myself.

So I'm dangerous.

To myself.

There's no one in the alleyway behind me. But it still feels wrong.

Walk on, slow, low, close to the wall down the side of Maple Street. Now there's nebs to see. Couple of old gobbos talking down the end of the road. One's leaning on his front gate, other's talking from the street.

Muffins.

But I got to stay out of sight. They're going to hear about me. They've maybe heard already. And this head-wound marks me out. Cut right down Wesley Lane. Worth going the long way round to avoid those gobbos.

But Wesley Lane's got more nebs in it.

Group of teenagers in the middle of the road. Having an argument about something. Three gobbos shouting at them from the pavement. Telling 'em to take their row somewhere else. Bit of lip back from one of the teenagers.

Stop, keep to the side of the road. Watch, wait.

More lip from the teenagers, then they move on. Gobbos do the same. Walk on, after the group, keep well back. They're still arguing. Big black kid's the ringleader. He's having a spix at one of the others. Power thing.

Who cares? Long as they make the noise and get all the attention, and keep moving. Which they are. Stay back, Bigeyes. Let 'em get well ahead. Follow slow. Keep to the side of the road.

More nebs on the other pavement. Old gobbo, see? But he's watching them, not me. Keeping out of the way. Another gobbo further back. Watching them too. Never knew gangs could be so useful.

Black kid's still mouthing off at one of his crew.

Going to be a fight soon if this goes on. And I don't want that. I just want 'em to keep moving, keep arguing till I can cut left at the end of the road. Headlamps down the street.

Slip behind the van, let 'em pass.

Walk on.

Group's close to the junction now. But they've stopped. Christ, Bigeyes, what is it with that black kid? He's still crabbing on at that other boy, won't gob up. He's got to move on, got to take his pack with him. I'm losing strength and I got to move soon or I'll waste up.

They're shifting.

Cutting right down Sedgemore Lane. Wait, give it a bit longer. On to the junction, check round. Gang's a good way down, no one looking back. Cut left, down to the end of the road, left again, right into Piper Lane.

And now we got to watch cute. Check round you, Bigeyes. I need you to be sharp, cos I'm not, OK? I got my brain in my guts. We're almost there. Just a short walk. But nobody's got to see us.

Nobody.

So check round. Specially behind you. Cos this is a cul de sac.

Get caught in here and we're drilled.

Looks OK. Just wish I was better in my head. I'm scared I'm missing stuff. But I got no choice. I got to get to this snug, got to rest. There's five minutes in me, maybe less. Walk on, down the lane.

All quiet, thank Christ. Usually is. That's what's good about this snug. What's bad is the old dunny who lives there. That's right, Bigeyes. I'm showing you a new kind of snug. A more risky one.

You've seen a couple of the snugs I use at night. And one of my daytime snugs. But they were all empty, right? Well, this is a third type. One where the owner's there too.

Only works with certain places and certain people. I don't like using these snugs. They're risky even if the owner's dimpy in the head. I only use 'em when I'm desperate. Like I am now.

But I should be OK here. The dunny's pretty deaf and she's got a gammy leg. Spends most of her time on the ground floor. Got her bedroom and bathroom down there and everything else she needs.

Proper stingebucket and a mouth like mud. I used to hear her slagging her lodgers when they complained. Wouldn't spend shit on their rooms but you name it, she's got it in hers. Bloody palace downstairs. Cop a glint through her windows and you'll see what I mean.

She's one spitty cow.

Lodgers have all moved out now. So I make use of her attic room when I got nowhere else to go. We got to be quiet though, Bigeyes. Back door and move soft, OK?

There's the house. Big old thing at the end. Light on, bottom right, curtains drawn. Got it? That's the lounge. She's probably in there with the television on. Let's go.

Stop by the house, check round. All quiet in the street. Sleepy place, this. Don't know if that's good or bad. Usually it's good. Right now I'm wary of everything. No sign of anyone watching from the street or the other houses.

No sign of the old dunny.

'You!'

Shit, it's her. Standing in the front door. Never saw her come out, never heard her. What's the matter with me? I don't miss things like that.

'You!' she calls again.

She's looking straight at me.

'What are you hanging around for?'

'I'm not hanging around.'

'Yes, you are. You're standing outside my house. And this is a cul de sac. It goes nowhere. So what are you hanging around for?'

'I got lost.'

'You're not lost. I've seen you here before. Loitering.'

I don't believe this, Bigeyes.

'Well?' she says.

I turn away, set off down the road. She calls after me, same bossy voice.

'Help me carry this.'

I stop, look round. She's disappeared inside the house but the front door's still open. She comes back, staggering with a big box.

'Take it, for God's sake!' she says.

I hurry back, up to the front door, take the box. Stuffed to the brim with broken crockery and empty plant pots. She gives me an imperious look.

'Put it round the side of the house. By the green dustbin.'

I carry it round, put it down, walk back. She's still standing in the doorway. Looks me over like I'm a dronk, then jets another question.

'What have you done to your forehead?'

'Nothing.'

'You've got a long cut. Have you been in a fight?'

'I got to go.'

'Wait there.'

She disappears inside the house, comes back a moment later.

'Lean forward.'

I lean forward. She dabs something moist on my forehead. Stings bad.

'Keep still.'

She glares at me and goes on dabbing, then presses a big plaster over the wound.

'You need to get that properly seen to.' Another imperious look. 'I've just done a patch-up job. You should get yourself to the hospital. And keep out of fights.'

She takes a step back, looks me up and down again.

'Now clear off.'

And she closes the door.

But I don't clear off. I can't, Bigeyes. I got no strength left for anywhere else. It's here or nowhere. Check round. No sign of her peering out, or any other nebs watching.

Round the back.

All quiet. Curtains not drawn in the kitchen. Check through the window. See what I mean? Twinky gear. She's not short of money. Check the back door. It's usually unlocked but I keep a nail under that stone in case I have to pick it.

But we're all right. It's unlocked. Ease open, listen cute. Sound of the television from inside the lounge. Pretty sure she's in there. Slip in, close the door. OK, Bigeyes, listen up.

Simple rules for this snug. We move quick and we move quiet. Got to get past the lounge and upstairs crack-smart. But we'll take some food with us. Apples, pasty, mineral water. That'll do. Let's go.

Down the hall, past the lounge, up the stairs. First floor, stop, listen. Sound of a cough from inside the lounge. Television still on. Up to the second floor, listen again. All's well. Check round, Bigeyes. Look at the cabinets. My other reason for coming here.

Books.

Cabinets full of 'em. Downstairs, both landings, see? She's got some good 'uns too. Worth the risk sometimes just to come here and read.

Into the upstairs bathroom. Turn the tap on, quiet. Splash my face, wash my hands, look up. I've been putting this moment off, Bigeyes. And it's worse than I thought.

Not the wound. Dunny's covered that pretty good with the plaster. And just as well. Must look a globby sight after shunting all that blood, never mind the other stuff Dig's knife ripped up.

No, it's my face.

I'm scared of my face.

I told you before about me and mirrors. I got to check my face every snug I go to. Make sure it's not turned so bad I can't bear to look at it. I'm dreading the day that happens. Only now I'm not seeing my face at all.

I'm seeing that gobbo's face. The one lying dead in

the storeroom. And now I'm looking at me. Like I'm dead too. I got to rest. Got to eat and drink and sleep. I'll think better when I've done all that. I'll be able to fight again. Live again. Get away.

Out of the bathroom, listen again. Just the television like before. Up the last set of stairs to the attic room. Books here too, see? Cabinets outside the room, either side of the door.

Romeo and Juliet.

Read that last time I was here. Book's still in the same place on the shelf.

Oliver Twist.

Read that too. Only not here.

Push open the door.

Nothing's changed. Same grubby hole. But it's got a bed. And the bed's got a mattress and a pillow. I'm aching to lie down now. But I got to eat first. Slump on the bed, grab the pasty, stuff it down. Same with the apples. Drink the mineral water.

Lie back. Try and sleep. Only I don't.

I can't.

I want to sleep so bad, Bigeyes. I want to forget, just for a bit. But I can't. Can't sleep, can't forget. And you know what? Sometimes even when I sleep, I don't forget. The pictures come to me in dreams.

The faces, the things I've done.

Do you reckon Scumbo gets that? Do his pictures follow him around? Does he ever get a moment—one tiny little moment—when he cares? I don't suppose so. He's like all the other grinks. One life on the outside, another life on the inside. He's probably got a wife somewhere who makes jam and thinks he's an insurance salesman.

I've seen too many like him. He's one of the old crowd. Nobody high up. Higher than Paddy's dregs, but nowhere near the top. He'll have known his pay-daddy but nobody else. Not the spikes who are pulling his strings.

There's a lot worse than him coming.

So why do my pictures follow me around? And why's everything changed? If I couldn't kill Scumbo or Paddy, how come I killed all the others? And how come I care? That's what haunts me now, Bigeyes. How come I care?

Close my eyes.

Still can't sleep. Maybe I should read. That usually

settles my head, except when the flashbacks are hitting too bad. But I need to sleep, need to rest. Cos tomorrow I got to run again, got to be strong enough to break free.

If I read, I won't sleep.

And anyway, I know the dunny's books too well. She doesn't keep the kind of stories I want right now. Like the one I read last year. Can't remember what it's called. Found it in a snug on the south side. It was a children's book with these wispy pictures. About a boy who stows away on a ship.

How dimpy is that, Bigeyes? I'm terrified of water but I love sea stories.

Anyway, he stows away on this ship, gets found out, and they make him work his passage. But he's a good lad and he makes friends with the captain. And then this big storm blows up, and the crew put off in the boats, cos the ship's going to sink, but they forget to take the boy with 'em.

But it's OK, Bigeyes. You know why? Cos the captain's stayed behind, so the boy's not on his own. He doesn't feel lonely. He's got a friend with him, a big, strong friend, who's going to look after him whatever happens. Even if they drown, he's got a friend with him.

But they don't drown.

The lifeboat gets out in the nick of time and takes 'em back to the shore.

I'm so tired, Bigeyes. Tired of running, tired of being on my own, tired of being scared. Like I'm on a sinking ship too, only I got no captain to look after me. And no lifeboat coming to take me home.

Just this.

An attic room in someone else's house.

But sleep's coming. Least I got that now. I can feel it. A beautiful, warm darkness. It folds round me. I'm dying in my head, Bigeyes. I'm blasted. I just want to dive deep and stay safe for a bit.

And I do. For a few sweet hours.

Till I wake again, trembling. It's dark, it's cold. The house is still.

But there's footsteps on the stairs.

Slip off the bed, knife open, ear to the door.

It's not the dunny.

It's grinks.

Don't ask me how I know.

Footsteps have stopped, halfway up the last flight of stairs. Hard to tell how many nebs. Definitely more than one. They're listening. Listening for me. Like I'm listening for them.

Back to the window, quiet, quick. Keep to the side, check out. Shadows moving round the back door. Two, three, four. There'll be more outside the front of the house.

And there's two at least on the stairs.

Back to the door, listen cute. Still silence. Got to wait. Got to hold back. They might just go. But I don't think so. They've come up this far. They'll check the attic room. They've checked the others. They'll check this one too. They wouldn't be here at all if someone hadn't seen me.

They'll come on. I know they will. But I got to wait. Just in case.

Still the silence. It feels like a mist. Buzz my eyes round the room. Nowhere to hide in here. Bad idea anyway. It's a simple choice now. Fight or die. Moment the footsteps start again, I'll know. If they head down the stairs, I stay quiet. Up the stairs and I blow. They start.

Up the stairs.

I'm out the door, knife up.

Two gobbos near the top. Never seen 'em before. They stop, fix me. Smooth types, like Scumbo, like Paddy. Only more dangerous.

'How you doing, kid?' says one. 'We heard you lost your bottle.'

'I just found it again. Looking at you dungpots.'

He smirks back at me.

'I don't think so. That's two in a row you've let go. First Paddy, then—'

'He got away, did he?'

'Oh, yeah. He got away.'

'How's his thumb? How's his little finger?'

'Healing nicely.' Gobbo gives me a wink. 'Don't know why you're holding that knife. Since you lost the guts to use it. Might as well come with us, kid. Breaking fingers and thumbs won't get you very far here.'

'Piss off!'

'Time to come home,' he mocks. 'Time to meet some old friends.'

They start up the stairs. I reach out, grab some books and fling 'em. William Shakespeare and Charles Dickens clock 'em in the face. I pull the cabinet, pull again. It lurches, tips, falls. And now it's thundering towards 'em.

Knocks both gobbos back down the stairs. I'm down after 'em. They're floundering on the landing but they're struggling back up. Jump over 'em, down the next flight of stairs to the first floor. Voices behind me, the gobbos yelling. Sound of footsteps running from the street. More yelling behind me. I'm on the next flight now, jumping down to the hall.

Dunny's lying dead at the bottom of the stairs.

Over her and off towards the drawing room. No point going for the front door. That's the way they'll come in. Door crashes open right that moment. Two gobbos burst through, followed by two more. Sound of footsteps from the back door.

Into the drawing room, slam the door, race to the window. I'm praying it's not stiff. Catch flicks back. Yank the window open, clamber out. Narrow path round the side of the house, fence straight in front of me.

I jump onto it and start to climb.

A hand grabs me from behind. Some gobbo's caught me from the drawing room window. Whip back with the knife, gash him in the face. He gives a roar and lets go. More gobbos crowd round the window. One starts to edge through.

But I'm up halfway over the fence now. Slip down the other side, stumble into next door's garden. I'm screaming now, top of my voice.

'Police! Call the police!'

Lights go on inside the house. I run over to the pond, pick up a garden gnome, fling it at the greenhouse. It crashes through like a bomb. Window opens in the house and a gobbo roars down.

'Hoy!'

'Police!' I shout. 'Police!'

'Who's down there? What's going on?'

I don't answer. I'm stumbling through flower-beds towards the next garden. Gobbo in the window goes on bellowing but there's no sign of the grinks. I reach the opposite fence, climb over. Guy's still bawling into the night and there's lights on all over his house. Run down to the bottom of the next garden.

Stop, think, just for a second. Got to crank my head. Got to work out which way to go. Can't just blunder about. The grinks'll have grouped and they're still close. They'll hang back cos of the porkers coming but they'll call more grinks and flood the area.

They know where I am now. And they know I'm weak.

They're right. I got no strength to spare. Fear did it again, got me away, but it won't keep me running for ever. I got to go to ground somehow. Got to stay safe through the night. And somehow . . .

Got to break free.

I'm so scared, Bigeyes.

Check round again. Still no grinks in sight but they'll be looking for ways to get past the houses into the gardens. They know I'm somewhere on this side. Harder to reach me with the nebs waking up but that won't stop 'em. Lights going on in all the houses now. I got to wig it fast as I can. Which way?

There's no good place now, no easy snug. Dunny's was the only one near enough. I feel bad about her, Bigeyes. I didn't like her but I didn't want her dead.

And they stiffed her cos of me. But I can't think about that now. I can hear voices from the houses.

Check round the fence. I know what's on the other side. Scrubby ground down to the railway line, building site beyond that, and then the houses start again. Let's get moving. Over the fence, down the other side, check for sounds.

No more voices but the distant wail of sirens.

Getting closer.

Move on. Got to move on. If I stop, I'm dead. I don't just mean the grinks. I mean the cold. It's fifty-fifty now. That's how it is. No messing, Bigeyes. This could be it.

Down the hill. Watch the ground. It's uneven. You can turn an ankle easy as wink. And we got enough problems without that as well. There's the railway line. Old signalman's hut over to the right. Can't shelter there. It's the first place they'll look. Got to go further. Think of somewhere they won't try.

Won't be easy.

They'll try everywhere.

Edge down the bank, check round, cross over the rails, up the other side, walk on. Getting colder,

Bigeyes. I don't like this. It was bad enough before but now it's getting worse. Can't be more than two in the morning and it'll be a good few hours before it gets warmer.

If it does.

Walk on, over the waste ground. I've thought of somewhere, Bigeyes, somewhere we can rest. And it's close. But it's bad, really bad. It won't be warm, it probably won't be safe. It's not a place to die in. But what choice have we got now?

See the fence round the building site? Walk up, stop outside, peer through. Looks like a bombsite, yeah? They're supposed to be putting up a shopping complex. Lots of nice warm buildings—only they're not here yet. So we'll make do with a pipe.

Yeah, I know.

But there's nowhere else I can get to now. We got to slap it like duffs. If I can just get the strength for this last climb. Breathe slow, check round. Got to be careful even here. They got a nightwatchman some-where.

But he's not very hard-working.

No sign of him. No sign of dogs.

Or grinks.

Means nothing. But we got to give it a go.

Up the fence, hand over hand. Least it's an easy climb. Drop down the other side, scramble round the perimeter, down into the ditch on the right. You're wondering how I know my way, right? I told you once before, Bigeyes.

I watch. I remember.

And now I'm glad. Cos this is our place for the rest of the night. And it's free. Down to the bottom of the ditch, into the pipe, curl up in the darkness, close my eyes. And now there's a new choice.

Sleep or die. Or maybe both.

And you know what, Bigeyes?

I don't much care now which one I get.

Only I'm lying. I do care. I can't sleep, Bigeyes. And right now I can't die either. Maybe it'll come in an hour or so. Right now all I can do is shiver. And think. And cry.

Why'm I crying? Eh? Why? Effing bloody tears. Who does that help? Not me. Not anybody else. They won't make me live. They won't make me die. They won't bring sweet Becky back.

Or that spitty old dunny lying at the foot of her staircase. Or the gobbo in the hospital storeroom. Won't make his missus feel better. Or his family. Or the others. Yeah, there's others I could tell you about. I can see all their faces.

I'm still holding the knife, see?

Scumbo's little toy.

And here's what I hate. I've been holding it all this time. But I haven't noticed. Like you don't notice you got hands and feet. Not unless you look for 'em special. Most of the time you just know you got 'em. You take 'em for granted.

Like this knife.

I just take it for granted. I remember the attic room, the footsteps on the stairs. I remember slipping off the bed, and there's the knife ready in my hand. But I don't remember pulling it out of my pocket. I don't remember flicking it open.

Maybe it was already open.

Maybe I was already holding it.

I don't remember, Bigeyes. That's the crack of it.

The knife was just there. Like my hands and feet are just there. And now here it is again. Blade open. Tight in my grip.

Look around you, Bigeyes. This is our world now. Darkness, cold, danger. A ditch of sand and sludge. A pipe. A knife that won't die. And tears. It's like I'm made of tears.

I can't get my head round that. Maybe it's just cos I'm ill. Cos I know I'm dying. Still shivering too. I won't get any sleep tonight. Might just as well get used to that. I'm going to shiver my way into Death's black heart.

And then?

God knows. If there is a God. I don't much care, you know?

Tell you why. Cos he shoved me on Day One. I told you before. That's when the trouble started. Day bloody One. I saw a bit of that picture when I was spooking my head in the ambulance. Or felt it anyway.

My mum and dad—whoever they were—took one look at me and said no. They might just as well have put me here.

In this pipe.

Only they put me in another kind of pipe. And left me. How do I know? Cos I remember the nebs who found me. And what they told me. And what they did. And that's when I knew there can't be a God.

Not one who loves me anyway.

If there is, he's busy somewhere else.

Anyway, it's too late now. I'm shivering my life away and I'm crying and I just want it to be over. But now it's all starting again. Cos I can see a shadow moving on the other side of the ditch.

Shit, Bigeyes, can't I even die in peace?

Hard to know what to do. Wriggle to the opening and check out if it's danger or wriggle further in and keep out of sight. Best to keep out of sight but if it's grinks and they look in, I'm plugged.

Got to check it out.

Knife's still tight in my fist, see? Same again. It's just there. I don't have to think about it. It's just there. Anyway . . .

Wriggle towards the opening, peer out.

It's a gobbo, middle-aged. And I know him.

Well, just. He's a muffin anyway. Sort of a dead-head duff who hangs around refuse dumps. I've seen him a few times. He's no trouble. Long as he's not looking for conversation. That could bring the grinks.

Cos they're still close.

I can feel it.

Christ, he's seen me. He's coming over.

Big brute of a guy, harmless but thick. I got to get rid of him. He lumbers over, stops outside the pipe, swaying like he's drunk. But he always does that. He's staring down at me, eyes wide, mouth chewing air.

'Get lost,' I say.

He doesn't move, just stands there, gawping, like he doesn't know what to do.

'Clear off,' I say.

He goes on staring, scratches his head, gives a sneeze.

'Cold,' he says suddenly.

'Yeah, it's cold. Now beat it.'

I gesture with the knife.

He still doesn't go. What's wrong with this guy? I got nothing against him but I want him gone. He scratches his head again, shrugs.

'Cold,' he murmurs. 'It's . . . '

He doesn't finish, just turns and slopes off round

to the right. There's more pipes that way. He's probably looking for one of those. Stick my head out to make sure he's gone.

Yeah, he's wigged it. Let's hope the grinks leave him alone.

And us.

I feel bad about shoving him off. He meant no harm. But it's too dangerous having him around. And anyway, I got no strength for talk. No taste either. If I'm going to die, I don't want the likes of him watching.

I want to be on my own.

Roll over onto my back, peer up.

Hey, Bigeyes, check that out. Night sky, just like it was before. Maybe I should stay like this with my head out the pipe, take a risk. I might get seen but I might not.

And I wanted to die looking up at the stars. And the funnyface moon.

I'll take a risk. Yeah, why not?

Jesus, Bigeyes, it's crazy up there. All that darkness and all that light. There's Orion, see? I recognize it. There was this book in one of my snugs about astronomy. Written by some professor gobbo.

He said stars are like people. They're born, they grow up, they get old, and they die. The silvery bright ones are the young stars. The reddy orange ones are the old 'uns. And they're billions and billions and billions of miles away. There's not enough noughts on the calculator to say how far away they are.

And our planet's nothing.

I'm telling you, Bigeyes, it's a speck of nothing. If it blows up tomorrow, the universe won't even notice. Time and space and all this stuff'll just go on like we never existed.

Cos we don't matter. We're nothing, you and me. Look up, Bigeyes. Take it all in. We're just hopes and dreams. And then some more.

As for the stars . . .

I'll tell you something else that gobbo said in his book. He said some of the stars are dead before their light even gets here. That's right, Bigeyes. Some of those lights have come from ghosts.

I could be looking at people up there.

And maybe I am.

Some alive, some dead.

All winking in the darkness. Cos the dead don't go.

I'm telling you, Bigeyes, they don't go. You could kill everyone in the world and they'll just go on winking in the darkness. Your darkness. Till you're dead too. And then all the lights go out.

As for the moon . . .

That's just a dead thing too.

But at least its light comes quicker. And right now it's brightening the blade of Scumbo's knife. Hold it up. Looks almost pretty in my hand.

Fold it up, put it away.

Close my eyes.

I've seen enough of the night sky. I'll keep the stars in my head, and the moon, and the knife. And the winking lights of the nebs who've died.

Dawn. I'm shivering, but I've slept. And I'm still alive. Why'm I still alive? Something's happened. I got a coat draped over me.

Stiffen, check round. My head's still out the pipe, looking up. Rest of me's huddled into a ball, frozen up. Knife's clutched in my hand, blade open. Don't remember pulling it out again. And the coat . . .

It's that gobbo's coat. The duff's. I recognize it. His heavy old coat. Squirm out the pipe, check round. Got a mixture of feelings choking me up. Scared cos I didn't feel him come close, throw it over me.

That freaks me, Bigeyes. Cos I always know when someone's creeping up. Even when I'm asleep. That's how I've stayed alive. Only this time, when I was freezing and scared and restless, the duff comes right up, nails this on me and I never wake up.

And here's the other feeling that's choking me up.

Cos no one's ever done that to me before. Slipped me a coat. Why should they? Why should he? I said I know him, sort of. But only to nod. Not like I'd help him. Not like he'd help me. I thought. Specially after I was rude to him.

I'm choked up. I'm telling you.

He might even have saved my life with this coat.

But I can't think about that now. I got to decide what to do. We can't stay here. We got to be well gone before the site crew turn up. Question is: where to go? I didn't expect to be alive this morning. Trouble is I'm still weak. I got no energy. Well, not much.

And I'm still shivering.

It's more dangerous than yesterday. Way more. First up, no darkness to hide in. Second, there's everybody looking for us now. Grinks obviously but porkers too, and every neb and his dog who's heard the news. Which is most of the city. It'll be worse than ever now there's been more murders.

Everyone's going to be grilling for me.

So where? I guess it's a simple choice now. I told you I can't stay in the city. She's been good to me but her time's over. So it's either wig it and play dead somewhere else. Or go back to the Big Beast.

And fight 'em where they don't expect it.

Don't like either choice, Bigeyes. Not when I'm blasted like this. Gut tells me wig it. Find somewhere else. It's got to be still possible. There's other cities, other places to play dead. It'll take time to do my watching, find my new snugs. But I did it before. I can do it again. If I can just stay alive. And get away.

Or there's the Beast.

And that decides it. No contest really. I can't face the Beast. Not in this state. Not in any state probably. So it's wig it out the city. Get through this day, stay alive, stay out of sight, slip away when darkness comes.

Start again somewhere else.

Far away.

There's got to be places just as good as this city. Big places full of snugs. Places where I can be safe. Even if I can't be forgotten. Cos that's the problem, Bigeyes. That's why I got it wrong before. Part of me thought if I play dead long enough, they'll forget about me. Let me slip away. And the past won't matter. Only I was bung-stupid. Should have known better.

The spikes don't forget.

So the grinks keep coming. They'll always keep coming. So my next place has got to be better than this one. But that's looking too far ahead. Right now we got the biggest problem of all. Getting through to tonight.

I got a plan.

Or let's say an idea. All depends on how things go. If I can walk for starters. And not get recognized. This duff's coat'll help a bit. It's got a hood. Got to be careful though. Dodgy walking with a hood up

when it's not raining. Porkers come sniffing straightaway.

So it's a bit of a bum gripe. Hood down and I'm
dung. Hood up and I look suspicious. But there's nothing much I can do about that. Have to chance it. See
what's round me and do what feels best.

Let's go.

Pull the coat on proper, do up the buttons. Feels
warmer right off, but I'm still shivering. Got to get
moving and keep moving. Out of the ditch, check
round. All still, apart from a cat climbing on the digger.
No sign of the nightwatchman or any grinks.

But I don't feel right. There's too many of 'em to
lose now. And they're still close. I can feel it. Over to
the fence, check again. Something moving in the bushes
on the other side, something black. A dog sniffing
round. Makes me think of Buffy for a moment. But this
one's not interested in me.

I start to climb. Dog turns its head, fixes me. I'm
halfway up the fence.

Don't bark, doggy.

And don't come over.

He doesn't do either. Just looks a bit more, then

lopes off. I'm down the other side of the fence, checking round again. Nothing moving anywhere. Even the dog's disappeared.

Right, Bigeyes. Before the world wakes up.

Round the outside of the fence, off towards the estate. I don't come this way much. No decent snugs to speak of, nothing much to nick. But there is something I want. If I can just get there. But first things first.

Food.

I'm desperate for food.

Head's thumping now and I'm aching all over. Still shivering, still bombed out. And I'm crying again. Can't stop myself. Something about that duff and his coat. I'm still holding the knife too.

Jesus, Bigeyes. What is it about this thing?

I've been carrying it open since I crawled out the pipe. Fold it up, put it in the coat pocket. Feels big and heavy, even though it's light. I'm going to try and forget about it. For a bit anyway. And I suppose I don't need to worry. If there's grinks, it'll find my hand without me looking.

Like it always does.

Walk on, hood down. But I'm checking round me dead cute. Still quiet everywhere. No nebs to be seen yet. Robin perched on the fencepost further down. Takes no notice of me. Walk past and on down the track towards the children's playground. Through the swings and round to the exit.

Check again.

First of the streets, but all's still.

Hood up even so. It's risky now. Got to keep my head down, face hidden. Walk slow, side of the road. Sound of a car behind me. Let's hope it's nobody. No porkers or grinks anyway.

Just a van, doesn't stop.

Walk on, cut right round the back of the garage, past the roundabout, over the bridge, round the parade of shops. And there's the supermarket at the end. Still quiet but we got to watch out. There's nebs who like looking out of windows. And there's cameras.

But I can't be worrying too much now. I got to find something to eat.

This probably won't work. It's usually only certain times when you get stuff. And you got to be quick or the regular duffs get in first. Not expecting much this time of the morning. And if there is anything, it might not be any good. But we'll try anyway.

Round the back to the bins. Open the first. Nothing I can use. Same with the next, same with the next. Last one's got a packet of bread rolls, well past the sell-by. Grab it and go. Out to the street, check again. Baker shop further down's got the door open. I can smell the bread even from here. Edge down, stop by the door.

But I can't go in. There's nebs walking down the street towards me. Students by the look of 'em, like they're coming back from an all-night party. I can't cream anything from the baker's till they've gone. They walk past, don't even notice me.

Watch 'em go, then check through the baker's door. But it's no good. There's two gobbos in there, working the ovens. Cross the road, away from the shops, down into the park, slump on the first bench. And I'm into the bread rolls.

Christ, they taste good. I don't care if they're old. I'm just stuffing 'em down. And now up and off. Cos this is the next stage, Bigeyes. Yeah, I know. Dronky breakfast, but there's no time to look for more. We got to shift to the next place. Grab what we can for the journey. And then hide again till dark.

Let's move.

But it's getting harder. Moving, I mean. Those rolls made no difference. Tasted good cos I'm hungry but no energy in 'em. Not much in me either. I feel like I'm dragging myself. But we got to keep going.

Out the park and down Kensall Lane. Hood up, head down. But check round you, Bigeyes. We're on the north side of the city here and it's a mean stash. Run-down estates, houses guttered up. No one but drug-pushers burning dosh round here.

There's factories down that way but not many. It's mostly pubs and corner shops, and gangs on the streets. Trixi's crew used to come here sometimes. Don't think the other trolls liked it much but she did. She liked to mix it with other dregs when she ran out of people to fight round her own patch.

I got to watch my back here. Cos everyone's going to be twitchy about the murders. And there's gangs on the streets who'll know about Slicky. And one or two who'll recognize me.

Cut left, down towards the primary school. Got to keep moving while the streets are quiet. There's only one thing I ever come here for and you'll soon see what that is. Cos we're going to need it if we get away.

That's right, Bigeyes. We're talking if. Cos I'll tell you something—we're in deep grime. The porkers and grinks'll be watching every road out the city. So I can't take any of the usual routes. I got to play it cute. I thought of a way out but it's risky. And with so many nebs watching, it's no dead smash we'll get away.

But we got to try. Only here's trouble already. Police car nosing down the next street. Just caught a glimpse. Don't think they've seen us yet but if they turn down our street, we're split. Check round. Primary school's nearest.

Over the wall and into the playground, down past the office, round the back to the prefabs. Crouch, wait. Sound of an engine, pulling up in the street we just left. Peep round the side of the nearest classroom.

A car but it's not the porkers. It's another car. Big, black, shiny. All I can see's the bonnet. But I don't like the look of it. Creep round the back of the prefab, check behind me. No sign of anyone coming. But they are. Car's not there for no reason.

Run to the wall at the far end of the school, climb over it. Front garden of someone's house. Curtains drawn, no sounds inside. Round the side of the build-ing, check behind.

Two gobbos checking round the prefabs. One of 'em's the hairy grunt. The fat man who killed Mary's dog. I recognize the other one too. Lenny, that was his name. One of Paddy's slugs. They're looking my way now.

Don't think they've seen me. But they must have done before. And they'll have guessed I'm still close. Lenny's on his mobile now. I got to shift—and quick. Round the side of the wall, into the back garden. Row of gardens stretching away to the right. Houses still sleepy, thank God. I'm just hoping no one's looking out.

Down the garden to the fence, over that, and I'm into an alleyway running along the bottom. Breathing hard now. Can't keep going like this much longer and I'm still nowhere near where I got to go.

Move. Got to move, no matter what. I can feel the grinks getting closer. I don't have to see 'em. I can feel 'em. I always could. End of the alleyway, cross the road, down the next alleyway. End of that, turn right, past The Jolly Abbot, past the football ground, into the next estate.

Bike in the front garden. Pull it over, jump on, ride, ride.

A mile gone. More estates. No sign of grinks or porkers. But they're still close. I know it. And now the world's waking up quick. I can hear voices in the houses, radios, TVs. It's like the dawn chorus of the city. Only there's no birds singing. You don't hear birds in the city. Just nebs switching on their stumpy lives.

And now there's cars moving too.

Early risers, nebs off to work, off to wherever. I'm keeping on the estate, crossing the quiet lanes. But I can see the main road through the gaps, see the big stuff moving. I don't need to be told where the grinks are. I can smell 'em. Police cars too, rumbling up and down. And now the thing I feared most, and earlier than I expected.

Copters.

Two of 'em, well up in the sky, but they're over this part of the city.

Dump the bike, creep up to the wall of the nearest house. The copters are getting closer and the sound's going to bring nebs out of their houses to check what's going on. Front door opens and a crusty old gobbo trigs down to his front gate. Guy next door does the same.

'Bloody things,' says Crusty. 'This time of the morning.'

'They're probably looking for that boy,' says the other guy.

It's too good a chance to miss. Round the side of the house, check the back door. It's unlocked. Slip inside Crusty's house. I'm praying he hasn't got a missus. All quiet inside and the gobbo's still by the gate. I can see him through the front door.

Two things I want.

Food and shelter till the copters have gone.

Kitchen first. Apples, oranges, pie in the fridge. Shit, Crusty's coming back. Close the fridge, stuff the food in my pockets, hurry down the hall, into the coat cupboard. Close it almost shut. Mustn't let it click.

Sound of Crusty coming in, front door closing. Copter engines loud overhead. If they've seen me breaking in, I'm plugged. And they might have done. They might well have done.

But the engines fade away.

Radio goes on in the kitchen.

'The headlines. Police are still looking for a boy aged about fourteen following two new murders in the city. One took place at Central Hospital where the boy was being treated as a patient. The other was an elderly lady strangled in her home in the Heathside area of the city. The boy was also seen close to the site of this murder. Police are warning the public not to approach the boy, who was last seen wearing—'

Radio goes off. Crusty gives a hacking cough. Sound of footsteps past the coat cupboard and up the stairs. Wait a second, then out into the hall and down to the back door. Looks clear outside but I got to be careful. Open the back door, down to the fence at the bottom of the garden, start to climb.

'You! What are you doing?'

It's Crusty. He's leaning out of the bathroom window, toothbrush in one hand, paste round his mouth.

'What are you doing?'

Another window opens, next door. It's the guy he was speaking to by the gate.

'Everything all right, Mr Lomax?'

'It's that boy! I recognize him from the description!'

Both gobbos stare at me. I drop over the fence and down the other side. Only now there's no alleyway to hide in. This is the main road and it's packed with cars.

I'm running.

But it's like in a bad dream. When your legs move but you don't move with 'em. You're trying to run but you just flounder and float. I'm starting to panic. It's like there's eyes everywhere now, watching from cars, windows, pavements. And here's the copters whirring back.

Into the underpass, through to the other side of the road, down to the shops, left into Castle Mews. Boy delivering papers to the house at the end. He's halfway up the path, bike outside the gate. Jump on and ride. No shout from behind me. He hasn't seen yet.

And now I'm round the corner, pedalling hard. I got a mile to go, Bigeyes. That's all. If I can just get there without being seen. Copters are still up there but they've moved over to the left, like they missed me first time. Up onto the pavement.

Got to keep close to the houses, not just cos of the copters and the grinks but the gangs. I told you. It's a rough patch, this. Trixi's old spitting ground. There's bad shit round here. And here's two straight up. Shaven-head dronks, blocking the way. Sixteen, seventeen, mean-looking dingos. I've seen 'em before.

And they've seen me.

'It's Slicky!' calls one.

I'm off the pavement but suddenly there's four more. They spread out across the road. I brake, swerve the bike round, pedal back the way I came. Footsteps pounding behind me but I got a head start and I'm pulling away.

'Slicky!' they jeer. 'Slicky! Slicky!'

Round the corner, into the next street, ride on. I'm so tired, Bigeyes, so bloody tired. I just want to fall down, sleep, rest, die, whatever. But I can't. I got to get there, got to get away. Got to keep believing I can make it, somehow. Right at the end of the road, on down the next street, right again.

Check round. I'm pretty sure I've skirted the dronks. Got to hope so anyway. Left at the end of the road. All clear. Another half a mile, on, on, on. And now stop, take a breath, think. OK, Bigeyes, look ahead. Little cluster of houses, then a park with some trees.

We're almost there.

Dump the bike behind the wall.

Yeah, I know. Seems like a dimpy idea. But I'm too easy to see out here. I got to get off the road and I got to do it now. Got to make sure no one sees me from here on. Check round, climb over the wall, walk alongside the road.

Keep low, Bigeyes, and listen for cars. We got to stay out of sight if anything comes along. It's a quiet road, this one, but not that quiet. So listen and keep listening. Here comes something. An engine, behind us.

Duck below the wall. I want to look, see who it is, but I don't dare. Got to wait, got to be patient. Car draws closer. Up in the sky I can see the copters circling. They're still some way off but that means nothing. Who knows how far those nebs can see?

They could be watching me right this moment.

Car draws nearer, slows down. I crouch lower, ready to run. Knife's out already, bright in my hand. Car stops, close by. Sound of a door opening, then a laugh, a gobbo's laugh. And a sound I know. Someone's peeing over the wall.

Just misses me.

Another laugh, door closes, car drives on. I walk on, listening cute. Here's the houses. Got to take this one smart. Cut round the back towards the allotments. They got high fences at the bottom of the gardens and I'm hoping no one'll see me from the houses.

Up to the first, check round. No sign of anyone but a sound of kids playing in one of the gardens. Creep on past, slip down to the allotments, cut over, out the other side, check back. Nobody watching from the top windows. Leave the houses behind, push on towards the park.

I'll tell you something, Bigeyes, I'm looking at those trees now and I'm dreaming. They're like a sanctuary. If we can just get there without being seen, we got a chance. Shit, another engine. Behind us, like the last one.

Only this is bigger. I'm guessing it's a van, and it's slowing down too. Duck below the wall again, crouch, wait. Something tells me this isn't someone coming for a pee. Draws closer, moving slow, then rolls on past and stops, just ahead, engine ticking over.

Doesn't feel like normal grinks. Can't explain why. But it's trouble.

Don't ask me how I know.

Engine revs up, van moves on, sound fades away. Peep over the wall. No sign of danger, just the park and the trees beckoning. Come on, Bigeyes, this is it. Copters have pulled back, no cars on the road, no nebs watching. We won't get a better chance.

Into the park, into the trees.

At last.

OK, stick with me, close. Cut right, through the little copse into the alders. We stay on this side of the park. The trees are thicker here. We got to be careful, Bigeyes. There's a lawn over to the left with a pond and a footy pitch. We got to keep away from all that in case there's kids playing. So stay in the trees.

Walk on, walk on. Just a short stretch now. OK, stop.

Hide behind the oak, peer round. See the church down in the dip? Battered old thing with a scruffy little graveyard? Right, now bring your eyes back and look straight in front of you. Little patch of ground. You could almost walk through it and not notice what it is.

But it's not just any patch of ground, Bigeyes.

It's the overflow graveyard.

And not a very popular one. There's only a few stiffos in here. But that's OK, cos one of 'em's a friend of ours. Come on. Over to the far corner, under the spread of the willow. Don't know much about the gobbo buried here. John somebody. That's all I can read.

And no one else seems to care.

He's never got any flowers or anything. But he's got something of ours. Think back to the little stream, Bigeyes. And the hole in the wall. Remember that? Can you guess what's coming? OK, watch.

Behind the gravestone, the loose rock. Only it doesn't look loose, right? Well, it is. Check round, make sure no one's watching. I don't normally do this in daylight. I come at night, for obvious reasons. But I got no choice now.

Pull up the rock, reach down.

You guessed it.

A bag of goodies. Money first. Quick count. Yep, it's all there. Twelve and a half grand. And some silver. Don't know what I put the coins in for. Yeah, I know. You're wondering how many of these little safes I got.

Loads, Bigeyes. I'm telling you, I got loads, all round the city. And there's not just money in 'em. There's other stuff. Remember the diamonds I left behind in the last place?

Check this.

One diamond. That's all. But he's a big 'un. Look at him. Feast on that, Bigeyes. This beauty's worth more than all the others put together. And I'll tell you something. There's somebody out there wants him back very badly. And all the other things I've taken.

He wants me back too.

Very badly.

But won't talk about that now. Pocket the money, diamond back in the hole, wedge down the rock. And now we got to get to our hiding place. Only—

Shit! Freeze!

Voices.

They're close, they're in the trees. Back from the gravestone, check round. No sign of anyone but there's footsteps nearby, and voices again. And suddenly I'm tensed up. Cos I know 'em.

It's the trolls from Trixi's gang.

I can hear Sash, and Tammy, and Xen, and Kat. There's no way they're not looking for me. Maybe that was them in the van. I thought they'd had enough fun with me but I guess I was wrong. God knows how they found me. Maybe they got a message from those dronks.

They're coming this way. Scramble down to the church. If I can just slip round the back, I can maybe get away. Up to the gate, check back. I can see some of the trolls now, moving through the trees. Don't think they've snagged me. Crouch low, round the back of the church, slump to the ground.

Wait.

Silence. A long one. I hate it. Stare out over the field. There's the lane we got to take out of here. If we can just get there. Can't risk it yet. I'll be easy meat if I cut across the field now. Got to wait. Got to be patient. And hope they go away.

Only they don't.

I can hear footsteps again. Other side of the wall, moving round the church. In a few seconds somebody's going to appear and see me. And you know what, Bigeyes? I suddenly don't care.

Cos I can't run any more.

I can't move.

I've come to the end.

Footsteps draw closer. They sound strangely quiet, strangely OK. I don't know why that is. A figure appears round the corner of the church. Stands there, looking down at me. And I find I got tears in my eyes. Stupid effing tears.

It's Jaz.

She's just standing there, looking at me. And I'm looking back. Only I can hardly see her. I got my eyes flooded. I try to wipe 'em. But I can't move my hand. It's like I'm frozen.

Can't think, can't speak, can't move.

Eyes clear a bit. She's still there. I want her to speak. I want her to tell me it's OK. Cos last time I saw her she was terrified of me. Only now it's the other way round. I'm terrified of her. A three-year-old kid. I manage to speak.

'Jaz, it's me, baby.'

She comes forward, slow, still watching my face. Suddenly realize I'm holding the knife. I've been holding it all this time, blade open, pointing at her. She doesn't seem to bother about it. She just comes forward.

'It's me, baby,' I say.

She stops, just out of reach. I lower the knife, let it slip to the ground. She glances at it, back at me. Doesn't speak. I want her to speak, Bigeyes. I want her to speak so bad. I want her to tell me it's all right.

'I'll never scare you again,' I whisper.

Voice calls out, somewhere round the side of the wall. Guy's voice.

'Jaz!'

She holds my eyes a bit longer, then turns and walks back towards the corner of the church. Guy's voice calls again, closer.

'Jaz!'

She reaches the corner, stops, glances back. I reach

up and wipe my eyes. She disappears round the side of the church. Sound of more voices in the churchyard, some of the trolls.

'Where you been, Jaz?'

'We lost you.'

'Don't run off, OK?'

No answer from the little kid.

I scramble up, inch over to the edge of the wall, peep round. Six figures moving off. Jaz, Sash, Tammy, Xen, Kat, and then the guy. I recognize him straight off. Riff.

The slimy. The guy who followed us down the lane that time, gave us away to Paddy and his dregs. He turns suddenly. I hold still. More dangerous to pull back. Keep still, dead still. He's checking this way, like he's wary of where the kid's been. He knows she came round here.

Don't think he's seen me. But I got him clear. Same greasepot as before. I'm guessing it was him and the trolls in that van. And I'll tell you something else, Bigeyes. They were looking for me. They still are.

No sign of Bex. Maybe they killed her. But they still got the kid. Look at her, Bigeyes. She's like a little flower. Beauty surrounded by shit. If they hurt her, I'll kill 'em all. If it's the last thing I do.

Riff's still looking this way. I'm starting to wonder if he's fixed me. But then Sash turns and calls out.

'Riff, come on!'

And he follows, like a good boy. Always was a flump. I watch 'em go. And I keep my eyes on Jaz long as I can. But then they're gone. Back to where I was, slump on the ground again.

And here's the tears back. She's done for me, that kid. If I was scared of the grinks, scared of the troll-gang, I'm petrified of Jaz. Don't ask me why. She's not my kid. She's not even Bex's kid.

She's dead Trixi's kid. And some claphead father who's legged it. She's got no one. Just the trolls and Riff and God knows who else. I can't help her. She can't help me.

But I can't stop thinking about her.

It's no good. Got to wipe this out of my head. Got to think about me, about getting away. I made it this far. I'm close to the way out. There's a motorway service station just over two miles away. All I got to do is get there, find a lorry in the park, break into the back.

And head north. Or south. Or wherever. I can do it, Bigeyes. I can get away from here. I just got to keep low, keep out of sight, and get to the motorway service station. So why'm I still thinking about Jaz? Eh?

Why'm I doing that, Bigeyes?

I don't want to think about Jaz, or Bex, or sweet Becky, or you, or anyone. I just want to think about me, all right? Trouble is, I can't even do that. Not properly. I keep seeing these other faces too. All of 'em. More than I can count. They won't blast out of my head.

More effing tears. Wipe my eyes, back of my sleeve. Wound's hurting again, thank Christ. I want it to. I want something else to think about. Reach up and touch the plaster. It's wet through but still on, just. But I got tiredness slamming me senseless now.

Think of the plan. Got to think of the plan. Forget Jaz. Forget all the others. Think of the plan. First things first. Get to the hideout. Eat, rest, wait till dark. Then wig it to the motorway.

Pick up the knife, close it, slip it away. Pockets bulging now. Hood up, slink to the side of the church, check round. No sign of anybody. Back to the overflow graveyard and into the trees. Cut through towards the road. Sound of a motor.

Crouch low, watch through the foliage.

Van heading back towards the city. Same grumbly engine as the one I heard before. And I was right. It's the gang. I can see Tammy sitting in the front. And Riff driving. Watch 'em go.

I'm thinking of Jaz again. She's sitting in that van, out of sight. And I can't speak to her, Bigeyes. I can't make things right. Come on. We got to get out of here. There's nothing left in this city but pain.

Cut left, down to the fence, check round. All clear. Over the fence, into the field. We got to get over to that little lane but we're keeping off the road, OK? We'll trig through the field and this part's best. Grass is longest here. But we got to play it cute. It's still easy to see us if someone's looking down from the high ground behind us.

On over the field. Pain's getting worse in my head. I feel so weak now, so full of stuff I can't handle. It's bombing me out. It's not just Jaz. It's all the grime she's making me think of. Don't know why. She doesn't mean to. She's just a kid. She didn't say a word. Just looked at me with those munchy eyes. But she's opened me up.

And I'm scared of what's inside.

Keep moving, keep bloody moving. Might help me stop thinking. Halfway across the field and there's the lane. See that wall? The lane's on the other side. Only we can't use it yet. Not in daylight. We got to wait till dark. But I know a place to hide.

Up to the wall, check round. No sign of anybody watching. Now we got to be extra cute. We got to stay out of sight. Nobody must see us, not a soul. We stay this side of the wall, and we follow the lane along to the left.

Just for a bit. The hideout's not far from here and we can rest there till dark. But we got to stay down and keep below the wall. It's a quiet lane but we're taking no chances. Not now we're this close.

On, close to the wall. Keep down, Bigeyes. Keep right down. Field's dangerous too. The grass gets thinner further along. But I'm hoping we're OK. Field widens as we go on and we should be too hard to see from the other end. Only danger that way is if some farmer comes sniffing about.

But it looks OK.

And now the field's opening out. Look ahead, couple of miles. See the rise? Well, the motorway's below that. This lane goes under it and the service station's a spit down from there. But that's for later. Now look just ahead. Bushes and scrub and then the wall bends round to the right, see? It's following the twist of the lane. OK, walk on, close to the wall—and now look.

Little hump-back bridge.

And a ditch underneath.

That's the hideout. Under the lane. I slept there once. And we can use it again now. Follow the wall round, stop at the bridge, check round. All's quiet, all's still. Except . . .

Listen, Bigeyes.

Birdsong.

I told you there wasn't any in the city. But I can hear some now. You got it? That's a blackbird. No messing. A beautiful blackie. And he sounds plum. Like everything's OK, everything's happy, everything's like it should be.

So why'm I crying again, Bigeyes? Eh? Tell me that.

Maybe it's cos I know deep down that it's not going to work. I'm never going to break free. Not really. Cos even if I break free from the city, from all the places I've ever been to, I'm never going to break free from being me.

I'm never going to be like Blackie.

But I still got to go. That's the crack of it, Bigeyes.

I still got to go.

Down into the ditch, under the bridge, sit on the rock. Pull out the apples and oranges and the pie. Wipe my eyes. And now that's it, Bigeyes. Nothing more to do. We sit here. We eat, we rest, we wait.

And when night comes, we're gone.

Only it's not that simple, is it? Never is. I can't even say I'm surprised. If I'm honest, I kind of guessed. Darkness has come—and with it a light.

And a new clutch of fears.

Top of the hump-back bridge. Check down the lane, Bigeyes. Not towards the motorway. The other way, the way we came. Trace back down the lane to where it meets the road from the city, then follow that left for half a mile.

See the light?

All on its own?

Just gone out. You probably missed it. Well, I didn't. And I'll tell you what it's from. A motorbike. Tell you something else too. Whoever's on it knows where we are.

Which means other nebs do too.

You're thinking it's just a light. Could be anyone. Nothing to do with us. Well, you're wrong. It's grinks. And there'll be lots of 'em. They won't take any chances this time. And they won't just be back there. They'll be all round. They'll be making a big, big circle. And closing in.

Can't see 'em yet. Too dark and no stars or moon tonight. That'll make it hard for us. Hard for them too but they got it easier than we have. Cos there's so many of them. They'll stretch the circle all the way out to the motorway, all the way round the fields, every direction, and then move in slow.

We won't see 'em till the last minute.

Maybe it was Riff tipped 'em. He was their screamer last time. He's probably done it again. Spotted me peeping round the edge of the church after Jaz. Made like he didn't, drove off, rang 'em up. Left me to 'em. And now they're taking their time. But they'll all be in place and they'll be moving already, snuffing the air out of the circle.

And all the hope out of my life.

Come on, Bigeyes. We can't stay here.

Walk, down the lane. Yeah, I know. You're thinking why not the field where it's more hidden? Cos it won't work now. Trust me. The field's no place for us. It's just one big open space.

Lane's not much better.

But there's a little hamlet just ahead. Cluster of houses and a shop, closed down. And something else. Something I want. Won't save my life. But I've given up on that now anyway. Keep walking, keep watching. We can't get away. I know it. But I want to see 'em coming. I want to see their faces.

Still no sign yet. Just the dark lane stretching away. Blackie's out there too somewhere. I like the thought of that. Wonder what he's doing. Sitting quiet in some leafy snug, I hope. Knowing he's going to sing again tomorrow.

There's that light again, Bigeyes.

Behind you, see it? The motorbike light. It's moved but it's still keeping well back. I didn't even hear the engine. Maybe I'm losing my touch. Gone off again. Only now I can see figures moving in the darkness.

They're here sooner than I thought.

Check round. Just like I said. A big, big circle. Out in the fields, all around. And there'll be loads I can't see. They maybe haven't spotted me yet. But they will soon. They can't miss. I'm dead, Bigeyes. There's no way out of this.

But I can still do one thing.

If I'm quick.

Here's the hamlet. Houses well back from the lane, lights off. Like the nebs inside know there's going to be trouble. Only they don't. How could they? They're probably just sleeping. It's old nebs who live out here. I've seen 'em. Well, I'm glad they're tucked up cosy. I hope they stay that way.

There's too many people died cos of me.

On to the little shop, boarded up. And here's what I came for.

The phone box.

Better be working. Open the door, check the dial tone. It's cute. Now I'm glad I had some coins in my safe. Pull 'em out. Not many but enough. Cos I'll probably be dead in two minutes. But I got to find the number first.

Push in some coins, dial. Woman answers, starts the spiel. I cut in quick.

'Give me the number for The Crown in South Street.'

'Which town or city?'

I tell her. She goes quiet. I'm watching the darkness through the glass of the phone box. She comes back.

'Would you like me to connect you?'

'Just do it quick.'

'There's no need to be—'

'Just put me through, can you?'

She gives a snort, but puts me through. Sound of a phone ringing, then another woman's voice.

'The Crown?'

I take a breath. Got to sound polite or she'll crash me out.

'Can I speak to Jacob, please?'

I'm praying she'll just get him. She doesn't answer. Sound of voices in the background, pubby voices. Then a gobbo, old, gravelly, Irish.

'This is Jacob.'

'I need to speak to Mary.'

Another silence. I try again.

'Please. I need to speak to Mary.'

'I don't know anyone called Mary.'

'Mary, Lily, whatever she calls herself. Tell her it's a friend of Buffy's.'

Yet another silence. Far down the lane I can see the motorbike light again. It's closer but it's just stuck there. Goes out again. I see shadows moving into the hamlet.

Hear a voice on the line.

'Blade?'

It's Mary. And now I can't speak.

'Is that you?' she says.

'Yeah.'

I'm watching the shadows. They've stopped some

way back. Pretty sure they've seen me now. They're just waiting. Gathering all the others probably, just to make sure I can't get away. Twist round, check the other way.

More shadows coming from the other end. They've stopped too. And there's more coming over the fields. Mary speaks again, quietly, deliberately.

'There have been two murders in the last twenty-four hours.'

'I didn't do 'em. But . . . '

'But what?'

I don't answer. I can't.

'But what?' she says again.

I still can't answer. She speaks again.

'But you know something about them? Is that what you're saying?'

Silence.

'Or maybe something else?' she says. 'Maybe . . . you've done something like that yourself?'

I'm frozen now. But it's too late. I can't go back. She's walked right into my head without me saying anything.

'You've killed someone,' she says. 'Haven't you?'

'I got to go.'

'Maybe more than one person.'

'I got to go.'

'Then why haven't you hung up already?'

I don't know, Bigeyes. Why haven't I?

Another silence. She speaks again.

'Why have you phoned me?'

'You said I could. You said you couldn't promise to help me. But you promised to listen.'

'I'm listening.'

Only now I can't talk, Bigeyes. I can't say anything. I don't know what I wanted to say anyway. Maybe I just wanted to tell her . . . I don't know . . . that I'm not totally, totally evil.

But maybe I am. Maybe that's why I can't speak.

'Blade,' she says, 'you've got to give yourself up. Are you listening? You've got to face up to the law. You've got to face up to yourself.'

'I've done too much.' I'm watching the shadows move closer. 'Too many bad things.'

'Then you need to stop running. Running won't make any of those things right. You've phoned me because you feel bad. Because you've got a conscience. That's a good thing. That's a hopeful thing. So now do the next hopeful thing. Go to the police and tell them all the things you've done, and take responsibility.'

More shadows. Too many to bother counting. They're all around me. A wall of grinks.

Mary speaks again.

'There were two things you were right about.'

I don't answer. I'm watching the shadows edging forward.

'The bungalow wasn't mine,' she goes on. 'It belongs to a family I saw going away on holiday. I'd just arrived and I was desperate for somewhere to stay. Somewhere secret where I couldn't be traced. I saw them catching a bus to the airport and made a note of their address from one of the luggage labels. I felt bad about using their bungalow. But I had to. Because of the second thing you were right about.'

'You're on the run.'

'Yes, but not from the police. From other people. I came to the city to find someone. I won't say any more. Except that I'm not a criminal. And that's why

I'm not being hypocritical when I urge you to give yourself up to the police.'

'It's too late for that.'

'It's not. Phone them. Do it now.'

'The only person I ever want to phone is you.'

I don't know why I said that. Sounds stupid. The shadows move even closer. Mary speaks again.

'You won't be able to phone me much longer.'

'Why not? You going away?'

'In a manner of speaking.'

'What does that mean?'

She's quiet for a moment. Then she comes back. Her voice sounds so soft, so Irish, so beautiful.

'Put it this way—the doctor gave me three weeks. And that was four weeks ago.'

Peeps in the phone. I crash another coin in.

'Blade,' she says. 'Go to the police. Please. Do the right thing. Do it for me. Do it for yourself.'

The phone goes dead. She's hung up. I push open the door, step out onto the lane. It's dark with figures now. No torches, no faces. Just scum, creeping close.

And then I hear it.

The roar of the engine. A light flares over me.

I stare down the lane, past the moving figures, and there's the motorbike, and it's a big 'un, a great, bellowing beast of a machine. I can see the rider hunched over, helmet shining in the night.

The bike thunders forward. It's close to the wall of grinks now. They're turning, bracing themselves, but it scatters 'em easy as it bursts through. And now it's racing straight for me. I jump back, press myself against the phone box. The shadows are moving forward again, but I'm watching the bike.

It squeals to a halt beside me.

'Get on!' says the rider.

A gobbo's voice, gruff. Can't see his face but I don't care. I'm on the bike, I'm clutching the rack, and he's revving up already. Now the grinks come running. I cling on, watching 'em loom close. They won't scatter this time. I duck, ready for the blows.

But they never come. With a growl of the engine we burst through and out the other side. And here's the lane stretching away, cut through by the beam of the light, and we're racing on, into the night, into a darkness I'm scared to see.

tim bowler

RUNNING SCARED

In the next instalment of Blade . . .

> This gobbo's trouble. Big trouble too, dangerous.
> You don't risk your neck like he did for nothing.
> He gritted it big time to get me away. So what
> does he want?
> Whatever it is, Bigeyes, it'll be messy.

My eyes are closing and it's like I'm gone. I'm not Blade. I'm not a fourteen-year-old kid clinging to the back of a motorbike. I'm not anyone. I'm just a thought moving through darkness.

I like that.

A thought moving through darkness.

The world's gone, life's gone. Blade's gone.

I just hope he never comes back.

Let the blood flow all it wants.

Cos you know what, Bigeyes? I owe it. Too right I do. I owe more blood than I got in my body. Maybe if it all drains away, I'll have given something back. Not enough for what I owe. Not by a long way. But maybe enough to get a bit of peace.

And there's something else too.

I'll be dead.

And you don't get more peaceful than that.

What's happened to me, Bigeyes? Has my brain stopped working? Why wasn't I ready for this? Cos I've been thinking of Jaz and only Jaz, that's why. Wanting her to be all right. And that's cute. That's how it should be. But what about Mary?

Why didn't I look out for her?

Tim Bowler is one of the UK's most compelling and original writers for teenagers. He was born in Leigh-on-Sea in Essex and after studying Swedish at university, he worked in forestry, the timber trade, teaching and translating before becoming a full-time writer. He lives with his wife in a small village in Devon and his work-room is an old stone outhouse known to friends as 'Tim's Bolthole'.

Tim has written nine novels and won twelve awards, including the prestigious Carnegie Medal for *River Boy*. His most recent novel is the gripping *Bloodchild* and his provocative new *BLADE* series is already being hailed as a groundbreaking work of fiction. He has been described by the *Sunday Telegraph* as 'the master of the psychological thriller' and by the *Independent* as 'one of the truly individual voices in British teenage fiction'.